## "*Now look, Logan.*"

"I am looking. I promise you I am. And remembering..." He let his voice trail away on a sensual depth that brought the color flaring to her face. "You aren't engaged, then? Or promised in future wedlock?"

Melly's eyes shot sparks that could have lit a fire at thirty paces. "You really have got a cheek, Logan Steer! How dare you question me like this?"

Suddenly all the amusement left his face "All these years, eight years, and you haven't mellowed one tiny bit. What on earth was it I was supposed to have done...?"

**HELEN BROOKS** lives in Northamptonshire, England, and is married with three children. As she is a committed Christian, busy housewife and mother, her spare time is at a premium but her hobbies include reading, swimming, gardening and walking her two energetic, inquisitive and very endearing young dogs. Her long-cherished aspiration to write became a reality when she put pen to paper on reaching the age of forty, and sent the result off to Harlequin Mills & Boon.

Helen Brooks creates special romances with an extra touch of intensity and emotional sizzle!

*Books by Helen Brooks*

HARLEQUIN PRESENTS
1844—A HEARTLESS MARRIAGE

HARLEQUIN ROMANCE
3350—AND THE BRIDE WORE BLACK
3378—ANGELS DO HAVE WINGS
3434—DREAM WEDDING

# HELEN BROOKS

*Lace and Satin*

## *Harlequin Books*

TORONTO • NEW YORK • LONDON
AMSTERDAM • PARIS • SYDNEY • HAMBURG
STOCKHOLM • ATHENS • TOKYO • MILAN
MADRID • WARSAW • BUDAPEST • AUCKLAND

ISBN 0-373-18661-4

LACE AND SATIN

First North American Publication 1997.

Copyright © 1995 by Helen Brooks.

# CHAPTER ONE

'WELL, would you believe it, Amelia Higginbottom! It is Amelia, isn't it?'

Melly stopped dead on the wide stone steps leading into the enormous office block as the mockingly amused deep male voice hit her ears like a violent blow and the pouring rain dripped steadily down her neck in ever increasing volume. It wasn't! It just couldn't be. Not on a morning like this when she had forgotten her umbrella and had had to walk the last few hundred yards to work when her bus had driven into the back of a taxi.

She turned slowly to confront the tall dark man who had been emerging from the back of a prestigious Bentley as she had scurried past, and was now standing under an enormous black umbrella on the first step, and raised her gaze up and up until she met the ice-blue eyes she would have recognised anywhere, the eyes that had haunted both her dreams and her waking hours for months until she had found the strength to put the past firmly behind her.

'Logan.' For the life of her she couldn't summon up the cold dismissive smile her new credibility as personal assistant and secretary to the chairman and managing director of Harp Hotels demanded. She wasn't just a pathetically innocent little first-year student now, she was *somebody*, but her brain refused to acknowledge the message.

'Logan Steer, isn't it?' Thank goodness she had retained enough coherent thought to put a question mark after his name, she thought weakly, as the tanned rugged face looking down at her maintained its lazy, satirical expression. It was a poor defence against that inflated ego, but better than nothing.

'You remember.' He gave her a smile that she assumed was supposed to captivate. 'Is that flattering?' His voice and eyes might be the same but the rest of him was almost unrecognisable, she thought breathlessly as she stared up into the dark features that seemed to have matured out of recognition since she had seen him last. How old would he be now? Thirty-one, thirty-two maybe, but he looked at least ten years older, the deep grooves radiating from his eyes and mouth and the thick black hair streaked with silver adding to, rather than detracting from the sensual good looks she remembered. As a young man of twenty-three he had been wildly and romantically attractive to the female population. Now he was devastating.

As her brain geared into action her smile materialised just as she had always planned it would if she ever saw him again. 'Possibly not,' she said coldly. 'Now if you'll excuse me...' The snub was direct and cool with just the right amount of disdain, and as she saw his mouth straighten she turned away smartly, walking straight into the warm centrally heated interior of the big office building without looking round once. She fairly flew across the foyer into the lift, not feeling safe until the doors glided shut and she was carried up to the immaculate hushed quarters of the élite on the top floor.

Once in her thickly carpeted, elegantly furnished office she hurried into the tiny *en suite* bathroom to inspect her hair and make-up. It couldn't be worse!

She surveyed herself weakly in the smart functional square mirror hanging over the small washbasin. Her thick curly chestnut hair was hanging in limp rats' tails that still dripped water, and most of her carefully applied make-up had been washed away in the morning downpour. 'Great, just great! I don't believe this,' she groaned softly.

She glanced at her watch quickly. Three-quarters of an hour before the rest of the office staff arrived. More than enough time to repair the damage and transform herself into the coolly efficient Miss Higginbottom they all knew, but that wasn't the point. Why did *he*, of all people, have to be on the steps of her office block on this precise morning? London was vast, enormous—it just wasn't *fair*! And that sarcastic mocking voice drawling the name she hated so much hadn't exactly added to her sense of fair play either. She glared at the fiery-eyed reflection in the mirror as she rubbed her hair dry with the small hand-towel. Logan Steer. Here in this corner of the world. The last she had heard of him he had been wowing America with his flair and rapier-sharp business acumen with, if she remembered rightly, his blonde model-type wife in tow. That must have been— she wrinkled her brow thoughtfully—five years ago now. But he was still as cruel and hateful as she remembered, worse if anything.

Well, she wasn't going to give him another thought. She nodded her head in a hard bounce as her dark velvet-brown eyes narrowed with uncharacteristic grimness.

She had made up her mind years ago that if she ever saw him again, which she had considered very doubtful, she would be cool and controlled and in full command of all her senses. Not like that last time. She shut her eyes tightly at the picture in her mind that brought all the sick humiliation and hot embarrassment flooding through her system as though it had happened yesterday. And then her eyes snapped open determinedly.

'But it wasn't yesterday, Melly, my girl,' she told the wide-eyed reflection sternly. 'You've grown up a lot since then. You are a successful career woman now, twenty-seven years old, with your own home and your own life. Forget that night and forget Logan Steer.'

It took a little more harsh talking and careful application with the hot brush and cosmetics she kept in the small cupboard behind the door, but by the time the rest of the employees of Harp Hotels were beginning to filter into the building her normal steady equilibrium had been attained.

Logan was a shadow from the past, nothing more. *Nothing more.* And she had been amazed that he even remembered her.

And flattered? The sly little voice in her head intruded with painful honesty before she had time to suppress it.

Of course not! She walked through into the office slowly. Why would she be flattered at being remembered by a rat like him? There was no consistency in the man, no depth, at least where his personal life was concerned. Apparently he was quite brilliant in the world of business, if all the newspaper reports were to be believed. He had the Midas touch, everything he was involved with turning to gold—at least that was the image. She smiled sourly. But images had a knack of getting tarnished.

What on earth was he doing round here? As she checked her diary and the notes on her desk, she found her mind was not on her work and grimaced crossly. She had been on holiday for three weeks, most of which had been spent decorating her small but wickedly expensive flat, and needed to pick up the reins in her usual efficient manner before her boss made an appearance.

She had got this job, over a host of other frighteningly capable applicants, because of her sheer dedication to work and her reputation for flawless competence and selfless commitment to the Harp Hotels empire. She worked excruciatingly long hours without a word of complaint or criticism, and in return had an immensely interesting and often exciting job with an enormous salary to boot. And if she felt isolated and a little lonely now and again? She squashed the thought firmly, horrified at its intrusion into her mind. She was lucky, very very lucky.

Right, Melly, *concentrate*, she told herself silently after realising she had read the same report twice without taking in a word. No more daydreaming. Giles Trent, her boss, would not appreciate finding her less than the well-oiled perfect machine he relied on so heavily.

As the internal phone rang, at exactly eight-thirty, she picked it up quickly. Giles wasn't in his office yet, which was unusual.

'Melly?' It was Giles's grating voice on the line. 'We're in the boardroom, six of us. No need for you to come down at the moment, but organise coffee and croissants, would you? We've been here since before eight. And inform switchboard no interruptions, all calls through you.' There was a second's pause when she expected the phone to go dead, and then his voice spoke again, clearly as an afterthought. 'Good holiday?' She made the expected bland response and put down the phone thoughtfully. What had been happening while she had been gone? Something important, if her intuition was serving her right. Still, no doubt she'd learn all when Giles eventually appeared.

It was just after eleven when she heard his voice outside her office, although the ankle-deep carpeting in the outer corridor made determining how many people were with him quite impossible. She heard his door open and close, the sound of muffled conversation and male laughter, and then her interconnecting door opened abruptly and Giles's iron-grey head thrust aggressively into the room. 'Melly? Come in here, would you? I'd like you to take a few notes.'

'Of course.' She rose swiftly, straightened the pencil-slim skirt of her steel-blue suit and picked up her notebook quickly. She had taken several steps into the room and was just preparing to sink down in the seat Giles had indicated at the side of his desk when Logan spoke, very slowly, and with a drawling, lazy satisfaction that caused her to freeze.

'Amelia. We meet again. I had no idea it would be so soon.' As he stepped out from behind Alfred Hynes, the financial director, her eyes shot to meet his. 'So you are the virtuous Melly I've been hearing about from Giles? His capable right hand.'

The word 'virtuous' had been chosen deliberately, she just knew it, and she also realised her earlier rebuff had been noted and filed for future reference. The silver-blue eyes were icy as they slowly wandered from her flushed face down her body in an insulting perusal that was intended to mortify before snapping back to meet her dark brown gaze. She stood, stock-still and silent, meeting his eyes proudly and without faltering. 'Logan.' She nodded coldly. 'What a surprise.' Her voice dripped contempt.

No one could have doubted how she viewed this particular 'surprise' and, as the other men present shifted uncomfortably, Giles spoke hastily, with one furiously incensed glance in her direction as he tried to pour oil over troubled waters, turning quickly to Logan with an ingratiating smile.

'You've met? How nice. Now, if we're ready, gentlemen.' He indicated the empty seats with a wave of his hand. 'Would you care to be seated?'

As Melly sank into her seat she was mentally kicking herself for her stupidity. How could she have risen to his bait like that? Giles would be furious, more than furious, that she had treated one of his business colleagues with such rudeness. She had stepped right out of character and no excuse, however valid, would justify her action in Giles's eyes. And there was no way she could tell him why the sight of Logan Steer was like a red rag to a bull. No way. What could she do?

'If you're ready, Melly?' As Giles's voice cut into her racing thoughts she became horribly aware, with a sick thumping of her heart, that he had been speaking for some seconds and she hadn't heard a word. 'Thank you. I'll begin again.' The look he gave her was one of fury tinged with amazement, and she took a deep breath as her hand began to fly over the page. Concentrate, Melly, concentrate. It became easier after a few moments as the meeting progressed but she was vitally aware, with every nerve and sinew in her body, of each move the big dark figure seated across the room made. With her head lowered she could just see his legs, stretched out in apparently lazy and calm relaxation on the perimeter of her eyeline, and they were an insult in themselves. How *dared* he be so cool and unmoved when she felt every nerve was ready to explode in a million pieces?

She checked herself and closed off that part of her mind with steely determination. If she didn't focus in on this shorthand she'd never transcribe it, not in a million years. Giles was not a man who suffered fools gladly, nor was he a giver of second chances. One gaffe was enough, more than enough, so whatever that swine

across the room threw at her from now on she had to
be sweetness and light. Even if it killed her.

'Right, gentlemen, I think that takes care of the main
points?' By the time the meeting was finished Melly's
hand was aching and her mind was racing. A new chain
of hotels in France with the first one scheduled in Paris
immediately? And *Logan Steer* as independent business
consultant? When had all this taken shape? There had
only been a whisper of Giles diversifying into other
countries when she had left three weeks ago, nothing
concrete. And suddenly it was a *fait accompli*. Why, oh,
why did he have to be involved...?

As the other three directors filed out of the room Giles
turned to Logan with the beaming smile he reserved for
those individuals more influential than himself. It wasn't
used often. 'Lunch, I think? Melly?'

She turned in the doorway of the interconnecting
room. 'Yes?' She kept her eyes strictly on Giles's square
blunt face as though her life depended on it.

'Table for two at Carters.' Giles's voice was brusque.
He clearly hadn't forgotten, or forgiven, her earlier
solecism.

'For two?' Logan's deep rich voice brought her boss's
eyes snapping to his and she forced herself, with
enormous self-control, to look blandly in Logan's direction as the fine hairs on the back of her neck stiffened
defensively. 'Surely you don't work the girl so hard
without providing food and water?' His tone was silky
smooth and infinitely kind and she could have kicked
him, hard, for such hypocrisy.

'Well——'

She cut into Giles's surprised voice as though she
hadn't realised he was beginning to speak. 'I've masses
of work to catch up on, Mr Steer,' she said with sugary

sweetness, 'as Mr Trent is fully aware. I've been on three weeks' holiday, you see.' Giles would never know the cost of the smile she stitched on to her face as she stared at Logan's cynical mocking eyes. 'But it was most kind of you to think of me.' She was hoping that the sarcasm which added a slight bite to the last sentence would only be picked up by Logan's ears, and from the small nod and smile Giles sent in her direction she presumed she had succeeded.

'How industrious. You really do have a gem here, Giles.' Logan smiled without it ever reaching his eyes. 'But it's been—what? Eight, nine years since we last met? I really can't let the chance of a résumé of old times be lost like this, but I'm only in London until tomorrow morning. Dinner? Tonight?'

'What?' Melly forgot all her earlier resolutions of convincing Giles she was back on form as she stared horror-stricken into Logan's dark face, in which the ice-blue of his eyes stood out in startling contrast to the rugged tanned skin.

'Dinner, Amelia?' Had he really forgotten how desperately she hated her name or was he using it on purpose?

'I'm sorry...' She found her breath had caught in her throat and took a long hard pull of air before continuing. 'I've a previous engagement.'

'Surely you can cancel it?' Giles asked irritably as he entered the conversation in his normal aggressive style. 'Who is it? Young Hopkins?' 'Young Hopkins' was Giles's assistant purchasing manager whom Melly had been dating occasionally for the last six months. At Melly's nod Giles nodded back dismissively. 'I'll explain to him this afternoon.' Melly stifled hot words of protest just in time.

'Shall we say eight, then?' For a moment Melly thought Logan's eyes were a shade colder as they glanced from Giles's direction and she had the strangest feeling, immediately dismissed, that he hadn't liked the other man's belligerent attitude in dealing with her. But that was ridiculous, of course. He now had exactly what he wanted. Why would he be concerned at the way Giles treated her, anyway? 'Your address?'

'I'd prefer to meet you somewhere,' Melly said hastily, as the shock that had held her stunned since his outrageous proposal receded a little. 'I've some things to do...' she added lamely. She had no intention of telling him where she lived, none at all!

'Of course.' His smile was very similar to that of a crocodile as it prepared to eat its victim, she thought grimly, as he held her glance across the room. He mentioned a restaurant that was renowned for both its food and the bank balance of the clientèle who could afford to eat there, and as she inclined her head in mute acceptance her eyes told him exactly where she thought he could go. And it was *hot*.

It was nearly three when the two men returned from lunch and, after arranging coffee, Melly applied herself to the work in hand and tried to ignore the deep bass voice on the other side of the door. But it was impossible. She sighed angrily after a time, furious with herself for the weakness, and more than a little frightened of what she had inadvertently got herself into. But then, she hadn't really, had she? she reasoned bitterly. It had been all his doing. He had played her as a master violinist played a Stradivarius, a virtuoso in his art of seducing women. And she had suffered that particular accomplishment of his at first hand.

Her mind winged back down the years as she sat idly staring at the neat signs in her shorthand notebook. She was nineteen again, nearing the end of her first year at university and full of righteous indignation at the way a final-year student had treated her best friend Lauren.

'I really love him, Melly, I'd do just anything for him,' Lauren had said tearfully, her huge blue eyes luminous with unshed tears and her mass of blonde hair shimmering in the artificial light of Melly's small room. 'I've never felt about anyone the way I do about him. And I thought——' she took a gulp of air and continued bravely, shaking back a lock of golden silk as she spoke '—I thought he loved me too.'

'Did he say that?' Melly asked practically as she poured them both coffee from the small coffee-maker she kept switched on all day when she was studying.

'Not exactly...' Lauren took the proffered mug and sniffed dismally. 'But he said I was beautiful, the most beautiful girl on campus, and that he was crazy about me. What would you think if someone said that to you?'

'I don't think there's any danger of that,' Melly replied with a little sympathetic grin. 'And you are the most beautiful girl on campus, Lauren.'

'I just can't believe he's finished with me like this.' Lauren stared at her with great blue eyes liquid with emotion. 'I've never had anyone do that to me before.' Melly could believe it. Normally the lads were falling over themselves for so much as a smile from the tall slim blonde whose beauty really was outstanding.

'Why did he do it? Did he say?' Melly asked after a long minute when they both sipped coffee without speaking.

'Not really.' Lauren's eyes slipped from hers to stare out of the window across a view of other buildings housing hundreds of little rooms like this one. 'But if you could just go and see him? Tell him I'm so upset? Would you, Melly?'

'Me?' Melly stared at her in horror. 'But I don't even know him, Lauren. I've only seen him in the distance a couple of times since you've been going out with him.'

'Please, Melly.' Lauren's lips, beautifully shaped lips, trembled pathetically. 'I'll never ask you to do another thing for me in my life.'

Melly doubted that. She doubted it very much indeed. Lauren had a habit of twisting everyone round her little finger, but she did it so graciously that no one seemed to mind.

'All right.' She looked at Lauren, resigning herself to the inevitable. She wouldn't be able to stand up against Lauren's misery and her friend knew it. There were definite disadvantages in having such a soft heart! 'Give me his room number and block. I'll try and call round after my last lecture tonight.'

'You're an angel, an absolute angel.' Suddenly Lauren was all smiles and dimples again, fluffing up her hair in Melly's mirror as she spoke and almost dancing out of the room.

It was just after seven that evening when Melly found herself knocking on Logan Steer's door and she had carefully rehearsed every word she was going to say. She would make it very clear she wasn't interfering, merely telling it as it was, and from that point on developments were up to him.

'Yes?' The first shock was the sheer old-fashioned sex appeal that oozed out of the man facing her in the doorway. It wasn't just the big male body or broad shoulders, not even the dark ebony hair or piercing blue eyes, but something else, something undefinable, that was disquietingly sensual and very, very earthy. 'Can I help you?'

'Er...' She found herself staring up at him like a complete idiot, and forced a smile to her lips as she took a deep hidden breath. She had never seen him close to before. In the distance he had looked...gorgeous. But now...

'I'm Lauren's friend. Lauren Grant?' she said weakly. 'I wondered if I could have a word with you about her?'

'About Lauren?' The blue eyes seemed to ice over fractionally, or had she imagined it? 'Why?'

'Problems, darling?' The female voice from the interior of the room was soft and drawling and as Melly's eyes opened wider she saw his narrow at the expression on her face. 'I've got to be going now anyway. See you later.' As the half closed door opened still wider a sultry brunette glided past Logan, after dropping a light kiss on his cheek, and smiled dismissively at Melly in much the same way a teacher humoured a small child who was being tedious. 'He's all yours, honey—be gentle with him.' She laughed mockingly.

Melly was still staring after her when she disappeared from view down the stairs, and then Logan spoke again, his voice definitely a few degrees colder. 'You had better come in...?'

'Melly,' she had said a trifle breathlessly.

'Short for Melanie?' he asked uninterestedly as he stepped back and she followed him into the very male room on which the covers of the bed were ruffled and drawn back as though very recently used.

'No, it's not, actually.' At his raised eyebrows she was forced to give her name which she hated with an intensity bordering on obsession. 'It's Amelia, Amelia Higginbottom.'

'Really?' For the first time since he had set eyes on her he really looked at her. 'That's a mouthful, isn't it? Doesn't really go with the hair and eyes.'

'It doesn't?' She realised afterwards she had been like a lamb to the slaughter.

'It's natural, of course,' he stated idly as he lifted a lock of her long chestnut hair to examine it more closely. 'And really quite lovely. So rich and warm.'

'Yes, well . . .' She would have liked to move away, but as he was still holding her hair she had no option but to remain in a proximity that was more than a little unnerving. Being an only child and having been sent to an all girls' school she had never really had much to do with boys, and since coming to university she had found her shyness positively crippling with the male gender. 'About Lauren?'

'Lauren.' The hand touching her hair moved abruptly and he turned away irritably, indicating the one chair in the room with a wave of his hand. 'Have a seat and say what you've got to say, but make it quick. I've masses of work to do.'

'Have you?' Suddenly the brusqueness fired the temper that went with the hair he liked so much. 'That girl was work, then, was she? I can imagine you've both been very busy.'

'*I beg your pardon*?' His voice was both surprised and angry and she swallowed deeply before continuing.

'It's just that, well, Lauren's been so upset at what's happened,' she said quickly as he moved back to her side, his eyes narrowed into ice-blue slits. 'She'd be devastated to know you've got someone else so fast.'

'Would she, indeed?' He crossed muscular arms as he stared down at her coldly. 'And what, exactly, has it got to do with you?'

'I'm her friend,' she answered weakly. He was so close now that she could see the small cleft in his chin, the thick black eyelashes ...

'Well, Amelia Higginbottom, Lauren's friend,' he drawled sarcastically, 'you are way out of line. What is, or isn't, between Lauren and myself is just that—between us. I have no intention of discussing either her or the lady who just left with you. Does Lauren know you are here?'

'Of course.' She stared at him indignantly, her cheeks fiery with a mixture of hot rage, humiliation and embarrassment.

'Ah, I see.' Something seemed to soften in the hard face as he looked down into her big velvet-brown eyes. 'She told you to come.' It was a statement, not a question. 'She would, of course.'

'Why of course?'

He stared at her for a long moment before replying, and there was something in the hard handsome face that caused her to hold her breath. She had never met a man like him before. And he was a man. Somehow he made all his peers seem like young boys in comparison. She felt a tingle of something hot and exciting shiver down her spine as he reached out a casual hand and stroked her hot cheek.

'Because, dear sweet little Amelia Higginbottom——'

'Don't keep calling me that,' she interrupted weakly as she moved back a pace. 'I hate it. Everyone calls me Melly.'

'Because,' he continued as though she hadn't spoken, 'your friend Lauren is as unlike you as chalk is cheese.'

'I know *that*,' she said with as much composure as she could muster through the mad pounding of her heart. Oh, she definitely knew that. If she had just an ounce of Lauren's confidence or beauty, this paralysing shyness would be a thing of the past.

'How old are you?' he asked abruptly as he turned away to switch on a kettle perched on a tiny table in the far corner of the small room.

'What?' She stared at the big broad masculine back helplessly. 'What has that got to do with anything?'

'Nothing,' he smiled lazily as he turned round to face her. 'I just want to know, that's all, and is tea or coffee your poison?'

'Tea, please.' After drinking endless cups of fresh-ground coffee from her little machine all day and every day she had developed a definite aversion to the instant sort. 'And I'm nineteen.'

'Nineteen . . .' He gazed at her with something burning deep in the arctic blue of his eyes that caused her stomach muscles to tighten. 'And as innocent as they come. How did I know that you were going to say tea? Tea and muffins.' His eyes wandered over her slim figure thoughtfully. 'And reading books curled up in front of the fire on a winter's afternoon. And cooking. I bet you like cooking.'

'Look, I don't know what——'

The deep rich voice was like thick cream. 'And you love animals, especially dogs and cats. Have you got a dog that you take for walks in the hills?'

'There aren't many hills in the middle of Coventry,' she answered slowly, totally bewildered by it all. How did he know all that about her? How *could* he have known? Suddenly she rebelled violently against his male perception. 'And I love coffee, as it happens. But not that sort.' She pointed to the jar of instant. 'I prefer real coffee.'

'Do you?' He dunked a tea-bag energetically in a mug of hot water, added milk and passed it to her, indicating the chair he had offered earlier with a little jerk of his head as he flung himself down on the bed. He hadn't asked her if she wanted sugar, and she didn't, but to her amazement she found herself asking for it just the same, just to prove... To prove what? she asked herself silently. This was ridiculous...

'What other surprises are there, hidden behind all that red hair and big eyes?' he asked slowly. She took a large gulp of the sweet tea without answering and stopped herself from grimacing just in time. It was like syrup! 'And do sit down, woman. You look most un-comfortable standing in the middle of the room like that,' he finished with a touch of the earlier irritation.

As she sank obediently into the chair she lowered her eyes from his gaze nervously. There was something, something almost tangible, in the room now. A thick heavy excitement, an almost painful awareness that she had never experienced in her life before. He frightened her, petrified her, but... She caught herself abruptly. Stop it, Melly, stop it. He's Lauren's, for goodness' sake, besides which he would never look at you in a million years, she told herself firmly. He must have the girls queueing for miles. In that, if nothing else, he was the perfect match for Lauren.

'Have you eaten?' She raised her head so quickly from the tight contemplation of her cup that a good portion of the liquid slurped over the side of the rim. 'And don't say "what?",' he added mockingly as her mouth opened to speak that very word. 'I was about to make myself a sandwich. Do you want one?'

'No thank you.' She was annoyed that her voice sounded so breathless, but the butterflies in her stomach were really going wild.

'No thank you.' He parroted her voice, but the mockery was gentle. 'Well, I'll do enough for two and if you want to join me...'

She was never quite sure afterwards how it was she stayed, but as it had grown dark outside his window the time had seemed to fly by. They had talked, laughed together, and she had found herself telling him things she had never told another living soul, and he had listened... It was with a start of real surprise that she glanced at her watch and saw it was nearly ten o'clock.

'I have to go.' She raised anxious brown eyes to his cool gaze. 'You had work to do——'

'No problem.' He smiled slowly. 'Stay all night if you want.' He finished the glass of wine from the bottle he had uncorked an hour earlier and poured them both another glass, his eyes tight on her flushed face.

'No, really, I do have to go.' Suddenly that earlier tension was back, but magnified a thousand times, and she felt horribly guilty as she remembered the point of her visit. Lauren. How could she have forgotten her friend so completely? 'Will you have a word with Lauren, then?' she asked quietly as she stood up, leaving the wine untouched. She had drunk two glasses and she wasn't used to alcohol; she could feel the effects in a slight feeling of muzziness in her head and a sensation of enormous well-being.

'A word?' He eyed her laconically as he walked idly to her side, his movements relaxed and almost cat-like. 'Any particular word?' He was close now, too close. As she stared up into his dark face she was aware that he smelt delicious and that something was growing in her lower stomach, something hot and fierce, that was sending thrills down her limbs.

'You know what I mean.' She tried to look away but found the power of those ice-blue eyes hypnotic.

'The only word I want to say to Lauren is goodbye,' he said lazily. 'She isn't quite what you think, Melly, believe me. I do know.' He reached down and lifted her glass of wine without letting go of her gaze. 'Finish this, it's a shame to waste it.'

'Logan——'

'Come on.' She took the glass from him because there really wasn't anything else she could do, and as she stood hesitating he lifted it carefully to her lips with his hand over hers. The sensation of drinking the rich fruity wine with his flesh warm on hers stayed with her for days after the event, funnily enough more vivid than that which came after. 'There is nothing between Lauren and myself, Melly,' he said softly as he looked deep into the rich brown of her eyes. 'There never was really, just a physical attraction that died as quickly as it was born.'

'But she said——' The words died in her throat as he placed a firm finger on her lips.

'I don't care what she said.' He smiled easily. 'She's already found someone else, you know. If you don't believe me, ask her.'

'I *don't* believe you.' She stared at him indignantly even as her body registered the strangest sensations.

'Oh, Melly, you're so naïve.' A slight trace of that irritation was back and then his face softened as he continued to look down at her. 'How on earth did an infant like you survive this long here? I know Lauren has found someone else because he happens to be a friend of mine, and the truth is she has been going out with both of us at the same time, in the fullest sense. You understand what I mean?' One black eyebrow rose quizzically at her bewilderment. 'Now call me old-fashioned if you like, but I prefer to think that when I make love to a girl she isn't warm from someone else's bed. My friend doesn't feel that way, fine——' he brushed a stray lock of hair from her cheek almost absentmindedly '—so I left the field clear for him. And *that* is why dear little Lauren has spun you a line. Because she isn't used to the old heave-ho, not because she cares about me.'

'That can't be true,' she said dazedly. 'She said she loves you——'

'Loves me?' The harsh bite of laughter made her jump. '*Lauren*? That lady only loves the reflection in the mirror, sweet thing. Love equals sex and it's just a game to her.'

She believed him. She didn't know why but she did. 'Oh, hell...' She stared at him dismally. 'I've made a real fool of myself, then.'

'Not at all.' He took the empty wine glass from her hand and placed it on the table, moving back immediately and taking her in his arms before she realised what was happening. 'But as you're here...'

She hadn't known, she had never even suspected, that a kiss could be so earth-shattering, but as her lips melted and clung to his she found she was trembling, helplessly, against the hardness of his body. Even in her innocence she recognised that his mouth and hands were knowledgeable—*too* knowledgeable? But then she was floating, aching and eager, as he continued to wreak havoc on her drugged senses. She was aware of him stiffening for a second in surprise at her immediate response, and then he drew her tighter into him, his mouth more urgent.

Later she blamed it on the wine, on his undoubted expertise in the art of making love, on anything and everything, but as his mouth fused with hers in a fire that caught them both unawares she was conscious that she wanted this incredible pleasure to continue. It was all so new, so thrilling, and with her senses dulled and mellowed by the wine and her body on fire with the exquisite sensations he was drawing forth, the thought of saying no hadn't even entered her mind.

'This is madness, absolute madness...' His voice was thick and hot and fired her still more, and as they sank down on to the bed together he buried his face in the soft curve of her neck, his breath warm against her ear. She wasn't aware of her light cotton shorts and top being removed as he stroked and petted her, her body arching at the delicious unfamiliar pleasure, but then as her breasts were released from their lacy covering and she felt his mouth trace a path where no man had even looked, let alone touched, she trembled quiveringly under his caress.

'Tell me to stop this...' His voice was muffled against her throat but she was incapable of obeying the almost desperate groan. She was just one dizzy, aching mass of sensation and she didn't want it to stop—ever. 'Melly, you don't know what you're doing to me.'

She wasn't aware of him removing his own clothes but then, as she opened dazed heavy eyes for one second, she saw he was naked, and fear and panic made her freeze. But then he was soothing her, kissing her, and the still small voice of warning was smothered.

There was something white-hot inside her which had to have release; beyond that she couldn't think. All the ideals and standards of nineteen years had melted under his touch. As he moved over her she was conscious of a moment's fear, violent and primitive, and then he froze totally before he could take her as a sharp knock sounded on the door from outside.

'Logan, sweetheart?' It sounded like the brunette of earlier. 'We've been waiting ages at the Union for you. Have you fallen asleep in there? I'm not surprised after this afternoon.' A low throaty giggle followed. 'Logan?'

The icy flood of stone-cold reason brought her scrambling from beneath him in an agony of embarrassment and crucifying humiliation, her eyes filled with such animal panic that Logan's face whitened as he glanced her way.

'Don't look like that.' He had reached across to her but she had flinched sharply away, tugging at her shorts and blouse with nerveless fingers. 'Melly, please. What on earth is the matter?'

'Logan?' The brunette spoke again. 'Are you in there, honey?'

How could she have done this? *How could she*! Melly shut her eyes for a split-second as she fastened the last button of her blouse and brushed her hair back from her face. She had laughed at all her mother's warnings about casual sex, the possibility of alcohol dulling the senses, of male opportunists and weak women. She had *known* she would never succumb to mere lust and attraction—she was going to save herself for Mr Right; she had *known*! And now, but for fate taking a hand in the form of the girl outside, she would have given away her virginity to a man she had known for less than twenty-four hours!

'Melly, listen to me——'

'Don't touch me, don't you dare touch me.' He moved to her side after pulling on his jeans, but she stepped back so violently she knocked her head on the window-pane. 'I have to go.'

'But you have to understand——'

'I understand.' She faced him tremblingly, her eyes black with vicious self-disgust and hot shame, two spots of vivid colour glowing like red wounds in the chalk white of her face. 'She's your new girlfriend, isn't she? You were here with her this afternoon, perhaps even making love. Although that word is an insult with you, it means nothing beyond the act itself, does it? That's how you think.'

'The hell it is!' He glared at her furiously. 'I admit I'm no angel, but what gives you the right——?' She cut off his deep strained voice with a stiff jerk of her head.

'Did you sleep with her this afternoon?' she asked flatly. He stared at her for a long moment before taking a deep cooling breath, and his voice was devoid of all expression when he next spoke.

'I can't discuss this with you now, Melly, you're too upset to understand——' Her heart sank into the depths of her being.

'I understand.' She stared at him with desperate pride. 'And I hate you, detest you, Logan Steer. Don't you ever come near me again.' She must have had a brainstorm, gone completely crazy, she thought wildly. This wasn't her, it couldn't be...

He didn't try to stop her when she walked across the room and opened the door, stepping past the sloe-eyed brunette outside, who raised knowingly mocking eyebrows as she passed. 'Logan, honey...' She just caught the other girl's voice as she fled down the stairs. 'What *have* you been doing to that girl...?'

He tried to contact her several times over the next week, but she had been steadfast in her refusal to have anything to do with him, her humiliation increasing tenfold when Lauren had airily confirmed everything he had said about their relationship.

'Oh, well, if he won't see reason he won't,' the blonde pouted the next day as Melly had flatly related Logan's words. 'Jim didn't see any reason why I couldn't go out with both of them; it's pathetic. Anyway, I've met someone else now, last night at that pub down the road. He's twenty-five and loaded, Mell—own sports car and everything.' As the blonde had fluttered on and on Melly had sat, white-faced and silent, and sunk in such utter despair that she hadn't heard a word. She had done all this, ruined her life, for nothing? Logan had been right, Lauren only loved herself...

After a few days reason asserted itself and, although the deep humiliation and shame didn't abate, the despair lessened. She hadn't lost her virginity on a whim, he hadn't taken her, even if it *was* more by chance than judgement, and no permanent harm was done. She now knew that she was vulnerable, more than she had ever dreamt possible, and she would *never* put herself in such a position again. She had escaped by the skin of her teeth, but he would be leaving the university in a couple of weeks and they would never meet again. And if they did? What then?

She stared into the mirror as she sat brushing the red hair he liked so much and which she had had shorn to a couple of inches all over the day after the fateful encounter. Then she would let him know that he meant absolutely nothing to her, *nothing*, less than nothing. She shut her eyes tightly as scalding tears ran down her cheeks.

If all the rumours her careful enquiries had revealed were true, he was a male stud of the worst kind, and the way he had seduced her, purposely and with all the expertise at his command, she had no reason to doubt them. He had wanted a few moments' cheap sex, and probably the fact that she was a virgin had intrigued him. She had to face it and live with it. He hadn't forced her, hadn't used brute strength, but this thing would be easier to face if he had. But he had got into her mind . . .

She scrubbed at her face furiously with a shaking hand. She hated him. Oh, she did, so much. And she hated herself too.

# CHAPTER TWO

'I'LL see you later, then.' Melly came back to the present to find the object of her wrath standing watching her silently in the interconnecting doorway. 'Don't be late.'

She glared at him, eyes narrowed, and as his cool enigmatic gaze moved over her face he shut the door carefully behind him and walked over to her desk, his movements still holding that animal smoothness she remembered from all those years ago. 'Do you still hate me so much?'

'What?' The direct confrontation wasn't what she had expected and it took a moment for her to pull herself together and draw on the aplomb she had nurtured so carefully for the last eight years. It had been easy to foster the cool untouchable façade, as it happened. She had never met another man who had remotely stirred her blood like the one in front of her now. Although he didn't any more, *not at all*.

'You heard what I said, Amelia Higginbottom.' The icy blue eyes stroked their cool chill over her flushed cheeks. 'You can be honest with me now—we're alone. You hate me, don't you?' he asked with remote coldness.

'Not at all.' She raised her head proudly as she brushed a wispy curl out of her eyes. She had kept her hair short. Never again would she let it grow long and thick to her waist as it had been when... 'I have no feelings for you one way or the other as it happens, Mr Steer. There is no reason why I should, is there? We're virtual strangers, after all.'

'Mr Steer?' He raised dark mocking eyebrows lazily. 'If we're going to eat together, shouldn't you be a little less formal?'

'I really don't see why we should eat together at all,' she countered tartly. 'You've got the idea I hate you, and I have no wish to dine with you now or at any other time. Surely those two facts alone should be sufficient to——'

'Such a beautiful colour.' As he leant forward and trailed a curl over his finger she forced herself to remain absolutely still when every nerve in her body was screaming to jerk away. But she wouldn't let him see he bothered her, never again would he have the satisfaction of knowing he could cut through her defences as easily as a hot knife through butter. It had happened once, but once was enough. 'I've never seen hair to match yours.'

'A little unbelievable, surely?' Somehow she managed that cool, dismissive smile that she had used hundreds of times in the past to fend off a prospective admirer. It held just the right amount of superior disinterest and always worked like a charm. Till now.

'You think so?' He leant forward with both hands palm down on the desk, bringing his face into line with hers. 'But I don't tell lies, Amelia Higginbottom. That, at least, is one sin you can't accuse me of.'

Just for a moment, a searingly shocking moment, she remembered his body naked and hot with passion, and then mercifully the door slammed shut in her mind so she brought the weakness under control. What was the matter with her? To think things like that in the middle of the office on a normal working day? But he smelt the same, that was the trouble, now he was so close. And it was delicious, sensual, expensive... 'I wouldn't dream of accusing you of anything,' she said coldly, her nerves going haywire again as he straightened slowly, the dark suit and blue silk shirt he was wearing accentuating the tanned hardness of his brown skin and vivid blueness of those piercing eyes.

'No?' He shook his head slowly as he crossed his arms in lazy perusal. 'What a dreadful little liar you are, Amelia.' He smiled but the twist to his mouth held no amusement.

'And don't call me that,' she hissed violently, realising too late she had responded just as he had hoped. 'You know I hate it.'

'Ah, yes, I do remember something being said along those lines, now you mention it,' he drawled slowly, his eyes lingering on the soft fullness of her lower lip before rising to meet her angry gaze. 'Well, I'm sorry to disappoint you, Melly, but you *will* be dining with me tonight.' He smiled coldly. 'And probably fairly often in the future, or at least the immediate future. I understand Giles has some good news to impart, so I'll leave you to it for now. Till eight.'

What was all that about? She sat staring at the closed door long after he had left, and jumped violently as the buzzer sounded right by her ear. 'Melly? Come in a moment,' Giles said in his usual abrupt manner as she clicked the button on the receiver.

'This Paris deal—you do understand you'll be required to leave almost immediately?' he asked as she walked through the door into his office. 'I shall need to be there for the first few weeks and I want you with me. Does that present any problems?'

'Er…' She stared at him vacantly. The world had gone mad since Logan Steer had re-entered her particular chunk of it.

'Well, yes or no?' he barked irritably.

'No, of course not.' She managed a businesslike smile as her mind raced frantically. At the initial interview two years ago Giles had mentioned the possibility of travel, but the most that had transpired were a few trips to the other hotels in England now and again, with a couple of nights away, and one brief weekend visit to Brussels the year before. But a few weeks? What about Marmalade?

'Good.' Her boss relaxed slightly as he nodded his approval. 'Alfred will be around for a few days, and of course Logan will be there. You two know each other, then?' The hard grey eyes had been curious but, beyond brief confirmation, Melly didn't venture any details and the working day progressed in its normal hectic fashion, with a brief visit by Paul Hopkins as he left at five.

'The old man said you were tied up tonight?' Paul ventured from the outside doorway after a careful check that her interconnecting door was firmly closed. 'All work and no play...' He wasn't really objecting and they both knew it. Paul had his eye on the main chance and Giles Trent was the big white chief; what he said was law. More than once Melly had had the unworthy suspicion that part of her attractiveness in Paul's eyes was her position as the chairman's secretary and personal assistant. Paul was serious and practical and very sound, and what was more, he respected her. She looked up at him now with a warm smile. He considered promiscuity in any form repellent and it matched her own views, forged in the fire of embarrassment and humiliation, exactly. He appreciated her mind, rising above the mere satiation of physical desire, and the odd chaste hug and kiss they exchanged now and again seemed to suit him admirably.

'It's not exactly work,' she said carefully. 'Mr Steer, a colleague of Giles's, has asked me to have a meal with him before he leaves England tomorrow. We'll be working pretty closely with him over the next few weeks on a new project so I suppose he wanted to break the ice...' she finished lamely.

Paul nodded cheerfully. 'No problem, Melly. To-morrow evening OK?'

Suddenly and quite irrationally she felt acute irritation at his easy acceptance of her dining with another man. How would Logan have reacted if she had done the same thing to him? Even as the thought popped into her mind she felt horror-stricken that she could compare Paul for a second with such low-life. It was to Paul's credit that he trusted her so perfectly and was never jealous or intolerant, of course it was, and she appreciated that in him, she did. She didn't want a man who was passionate and volatile and difficult. Paul was her ideal match, *of course* he was.

Later that evening, as she frantically discarded dress after dress until the huge pile on her bed left her wardrobe virtually empty, the thought intruded that she had never, ever, worried about what to wear for Paul. She stopped abruptly, the present dress falling in a silky heap at her feet as she stared at herself in the full-length mirror in her pretty bedroom.

She didn't like what she saw. Her eyes were bright, her cheeks flushed, and her hair tousled and soft about her face. It wasn't the cool, controlled face of the woman she had lived with for the last eight years. In fact it bore a sickening resemblance to the young, innocent girl of nineteen who had had her world invaded so callously.

She cut the thought grimly. She had to be calm and businesslike about all this, especially in view of Logan's present power and authority. He had crushed her once and it had taken a long, long time for the scars to heal. She wasn't about to let him spoil her life for a second time. She loathed him, had nothing but contempt and disgust for him, but for the moment she had to be practical. Her job was vitally important to her and she didn't intend to jeopardise it for him or anyone else. She could be civil for just a few weeks, play him at his own game maybe, but her thoughts would be her own. And at the end of that time she would still have her job, her flat, and Paul... Strangely, the little pep talk didn't give her the boost she needed.

She gathered up the cream silk dress slowly, fitting it over her slender hips and sliding the zip closed firmly. She wouldn't try another thing on. This would do. *Anything* would have done. She reached for the matching knee-length jacket, pulling it savagely off the hanger, her eyes fiery with self-contempt, and then subsided on the bed with a little moan.

'How am I going to get through this?' she asked the empty room weakly. She had never envisaged, in those odd few moments when she had allowed herself to think of him at all, that meeting him again would be like this. She had imagined a chance meeting in a crowded street or store, maybe a social function, and herself cool and triumphant, walking away with her head held high as Logan stared after her, suitably chastened at the new ice-cool woman she had become.

And what about his wife? The thought hit her mind like a ton of bricks. Did she encourage her husband to take secretaries out for dinner whenever he felt the inclination? She twisted painfully on the bed. But maybe

they had one of those so-called 'open' marriages?
Everything was permissible as long as it was discreet and
tasteful? She could imagine him insisting on something
like that. Her lip curled in distaste. Yes, she could just
imagine that...

A slight scratching on her bedroom window brought
her eyes snapping to the closed curtains, and after
drawing them aside she saw Marmalade sitting in quiet
contemplation on the windowsill outside, his huge green-
grey eyes surveying her unblinkingly. It had been a huge
bonus to get the bottom-floor flat in the old terraced
house in which she lived. The view from both her
bedroom and small living-room was directly on to the
long narrow lawned garden with its neat border of trees
and shrubs, and she had felt it was quite literally a little
oasis in the crowded busy city. When she had ap-
proached the landlord about keeping a pet he had been
less than enthusiastic, agreeing eventually that one cat,
'just one, mind,' would be acceptable.

And so Marmalade had made his appearance in her
life. A little scrap of ginger fur and enormous green eyes,
rescued by a little old lady some streets away from a
cardboard box dumped in an alley and passed on to
Melly via a notice in the local laundry. And he had
grown. And grown. At two years old he was the epitome
of the leader of the pack, often battle-scarred but always
victorious and with an undeniable air of satisfaction with
life.

He had transformed the small flat into a home overnight. Her parents had died within months of each other
just after she came to London, and she had missed their
company and that of the assortment of dogs and cats
she had grown up with more than she had thought

possible in those first early days by herself. So Marmalade was more than just a cat. He was family.

She opened the window and he jumped immediately into the room, winding his large body round her legs in greeting before marching to the closed door with an imperious miaow.

'I know, I know, dinnertime.' She surveyed him thoughtfully as he ate. He was another problem she had to solve in the next few days. She had overcome the odd overnight absence in the past with a litter tray and a good supply of dried food, but a few weeks? Her brow wrinkled reflectively. There was no one to have him. Paul would have been the ideal solution, but Marmalade had taken an instant and unreasonable dislike to him on their first meeting which Paul reciprocated in full, and the two barely tolerated each other.

Still, she had to go. She glanced at her watch and flew into the bedroom for one final check in the mirror. She had renewed her light make-up earlier and now, after running a comb through her soft red curls, heard the doorbell announce the arrival of the taxi outside. This was it. She took a deep breath as her heart pounded violently. Why had she ever agreed...?

'Melly.' As Logan rose at her approach Melly forced herself to continue walking at the same cool pace, but it had been a nasty moment. He looked so *gorgeous*. The dark business suit had gone and in its place the big body was clothed in an exquisitely cut light grey suit that shouted a designer label and, when teamed with the dull red silk shirt and tie that he wore with such casual ease, the whole effect was one of uncompromising sex appeal. Which he would be only too aware of, she thought nastily.

'Hello, Logan.' She smiled carefully, acutely aware that at least four or five pairs of female eyes were watching her with unconcealed envy. The tall lithe body, arrogant good looks and devastatingly insolent disregard of his surroundings were guaranteed to have the women falling over themselves to be noticed. It was a technique that was all the more effective for its apparent naturalness but—she looked him full in the face as she sank into the seat which the waiter had pulled out deferentially—she wasn't fooled for a minute. A wolf was a wolf, however its claws were trimmed or fur coiffured.

'I thought we'd have a cocktail before we go through,' Logan said smoothly as he met the hostile brown of her eyes. 'Champagne fizz all right?'

'Fine.' She smiled coolly. She had never tasted a champagne fizz in her life, but would walk through coals of fire before she admitted that to him.

As the waiter disappeared, almost gliding over to the bar, she looked up to find Logan's gaze tight on her face. 'You look lovely.'

'Thank you.' She didn't smile again. Two smiles in as many minutes was pushing his luck beyond the pale anyway.

'Although all that armour is going to prove a little wearing by the end of the evening.'

'Sorry?' She stared at him in surprise.

'"Young Hopins" is obviously made of stern stuff,' he continued with a dry smoothness that twanged her over-tight nerves like a badly strung guitar. 'Do you glare at him quite so ferociously?'

'Now look, Logan——'

'I am looking, I promise you I am. And remembering...' He let his voice trail away on a sensual depth that brought the colour flaring into her face. 'Eight years is a long time.'

'Not long enough,' she said tightly as the glare he had mentioned deepened. 'In fact a lifetime wouldn't be long enough...' She caught herself abruptly. This wasn't how she had planned it! She had been going to be cool and very composed, setting the ground rules for the next few weeks of close contact. She bit on her lower lip angrily. And instead he had made her lose her temper in the first thirty seconds!

'Your face is still a dead giveaway.' The mocking amused voice held a tinge of laziness that was incredibly galling in the circumstances. 'Transparent almost. I was worried the world might have hardened you——'

'Let's just leave the world out of this,' she said grimly. 'As far as I'm concerned——'

The waiter arriving with the cocktails brought her voice to an abrupt halt, and as she smiled her thanks and took a long sip of the bright pink liquid in the huge fluted glass she reminded herself, again, that losing her temper was fatal where this man was concerned. She forced her eyes to move round the small cocktail bar, situated just outside the massive dining-room visible through glass doors, as her heartbeat returned to normal. Nice and cool, Melly, she told herself tensely, nice and cool. Show this rat in human form that he doesn't touch you one iota.

'Who exactly is young Hopkins anyway?' Logan asked mildly after a full minute had ticked by in screaming silence. 'I presume he works for Giles too?'

'Paul is the assistant purchasing manager,' she said quietly as her eyes met his, 'and please stop calling him young Hopkins. He's twenty-eight, as it happens.'

'Twenty-eight?' His eyes stroked over her face thoughtfully. 'Paul Hopkins. Mrs Amelia Hopkins. No, I'm sorry, Melly, it just doesn't go.' He settled back in his seat lazily. 'It's hardly an improvement on Higginbott**om**.'

'I don't know what you're talking about,' she said with stiff formality as her eyes shot sparks that could have lit a fire at thirty paces. 'And leave my name out of this.'

'No?' He stretched out his long legs as he drained his glass. 'You aren't engaged, then? Or promised in future wedlock?'

'I don't consider that my private life is any business of yours,' she said tightly. 'And you really have got a cheek, Logan Steer! How dare you question me like this——?'

'Well, you know me . . .' He straightened in his seat and suddenly all amusement had left his dark face, leaving only a cold grimness that was more than a little unnerving. 'Unprincipled, degenerate, lacking even the most basic normal human decency. That's how you see me, isn't it?' It was a statement, not a question, and she stared at him silently without moving.

'All these years, eight years, and you haven't mellowed one tiny bit. What on earth was it I was supposed to have done, anyway? I admit I was stupid, that I hurried things a bit, but from my recollection you were there every inch of the way——'

'You rotten swine.' Her voice was a low hiss, but filled with such rage that it effectively silenced his. 'You seduced me. You know full well you seduced me. I didn't have a clue what was going on but you, you were sleeping with women by the score and I was very nearly just another number on your list! You *knew* what you were doing that night——'

'Of course I did.' Now his eyes were blazing back at hers with sheer fury. 'And where the hell you got the "score" from I don't know—the beauty of over-active imaginations and the local gossip-vine, I guess? And as for seducing you...' He stopped abruptly. 'Well, maybe I did. But not intentionally in the way you seem to think. That evening just sort of happened—you were there, dammit, you *know* that.'

'Oh, I know it all right,' she said grimly. 'And I also know exactly what was in your mind both then and now. You are a man who has to dominate, aren't you, has to know he can have any woman he wants whenever he wants? You aren't unique, Logan, there are a lot of others out there just like you.'

'Are there indeed?' He surveyed her angrily for one long, tense moment before relaxing back in his seat again with a deep, hard sigh. 'Are there indeed? And here was I thinking I was inimitable.'

'It's not funny.' She would have thrown her empty glass at his head if they had been anywhere else. How dared he take this so lightly?

'Damn right it's not.' He looked up suddenly and the coldness of the diamond-hard blue eyes told her that her words had hit deeper than she had thought. 'I can assure you the emotion which currently has us in its grip is not one of mirth, Melly. You are the most infuriating woman I have ever met! You were eight years ago and you are worse now, if anything. Why I'm bothering——'

The waiter had appeared at their side again and Logan ordered two more cocktails without consulting her by word or look, before asking if their table in the restaurant was ready.

'Certainly, Mr Steer.' The waiter was all smiles and nods. 'Your usual table, of course, sir. If you'd like to go through I'll bring the drinks straight over.'

Usual table? She kept her face blank.

As she stood up Logan gripped her elbow in a hold that was more punishing than guiding, leading her out of the small cocktail bar and through the massive glass doors that opened automatically at their approach. He led her straight to a table for two in the far corner of the beautifully and expensively furnished room and Melly was seated before she had time to draw breath. In the next instant the drinks were at their elbows and a menu had been placed in front of her. She felt a slight sense of unreality at the smoothness of it all. How the other half lived!

'Give us a moment, would you?' Logan asked the waiter unsmilingly.

'Certainly, Mr Steer.' They were alone the next second.

'Are you hungry?' Logan's ice-blue gaze was fixed firmly on her flushed face and she stared at him weakly as the piercing eyes bored into hers. 'I said, are you hungry?' he repeated with bland quietness.

'Yes.' It was true. To her amazement she found she was.

'Then can I suggest a truce,' he asked smoothly, 'just while we eat, of course? The restaurant Giles used at lunchtime, although adequate, gave portions more suited to an infants' tea party than filling a grown man's stomach and I am quite ravenous. The food here is superb and needs to be savoured course by course, you understand me?' She nodded silently. 'So... truce?' He smiled suddenly and she caught her breath deep in her throat. She remembered that smile from eight years ago. It had been wonderful then.

'Yes, all right.' For a second the most ridiculous notion that she wanted to burst into tears brought the blood rushing into her face. 'Truce.'

'Good.' He gave a sigh of deep satisfaction and turned to the menu, consulting with her on each course as he spoke to the waiter who had popped up again like the proverbial cork out of a bottle. Everyone seemed to know him. She looked at him silently as he acknowledged yet another signal from across the room, the third in as many minutes. It shouldn't annoy her but it did. And she wasn't quite sure why. And that annoyed her still more. And there was still the problem of Marmalade to sort out before she left for France. Oh, why was everything so difficult suddenly?

'I thought we'd agreed on a truce?' His voice was silky soft but it penetrated her thoughts immediately as her velvet-brown eyes focused on the steel-blue of his.

'I'm sorry.' She smiled uncertainly. 'I was just thinking.'

'Yes, I know.' He eyed her grimly. 'About me. I could tell.'

'Well, no, about my cat actually.'

He stared at her as though she was mad. 'Your cat?' He shook his head slowly. 'You did say your cat?' At her stiff nod, that devastating smile flashed for a brief moment in wry humour that gave her a queer little dart of something in her chest that felt suspiciously like pain. 'An ego-booster you surely aren't, Miss Amelia Higginbottom.' For the first time in her life the sound of her name didn't grate like barbed wire, maybe because she had never heard it spoken with such husky tenderness before. But that was crazy! She stared at him warily. She had been mistaken. Of course she had. The cold, enigmatic, handsome face that stared back at her was expressionless. 'If it's not a stupid question, why exactly were you thinking of your cat at a time when you should be smitten by my undoubted charms?' he asked drily.

'Oh, it's not your problem...' She waved a dismissive hand as the wine waiter appeared with the horribly expensive bottle Logan had ordered. Of course it tasted like all the delicious things she had ever drunk rolled into one. It had to, didn't it? *He* had ordered it. And he would know all the right wines after all, they were an essential tool in the seduction game.

'Your cat?' He returned to the attack once the waiter had left.

She stared at him guardedly. Now she'd mentioned Marmalade she had better explain. It was pretty safe territory, after all. As she described her dilemma she could see he didn't feel the situation merited the thought she was giving it. 'But there are places for animals, aren't there?' he asked lightly. 'Kennels or something?'

'Catteries.' She eyed him tightly. 'And there is no way I'm putting Marmalade somewhere like that.'

'Marmalade?' He shut his eyes for a split-second. 'Don't tell me, it's a ginger tom.'

'How did you know?' She carried on without waiting for a reply. 'Marmalade hates being confined. He's a very independent cat with a mind of his own.'

'Like mistress, like...' He let his voice fade as the glare returned. 'OK, so Marmalade doesn't like being shut in and you have to leave the country for a few weeks. Problem resolved. He can stay at my house.'

'Your house?' She cleared her throat and hoped her voice sounded less of a squeak. 'What do you mean, your house?'

'I *do* live in a house,' he said silkily, 'although I have to accept you probably assume I leave my coffin in the bowels of the earth somewhere to prowl the earth until my lust for flesh is satisfied——'

'Don't be ridiculous.' She tried for cool hauteur but it didn't quite come off. 'I couldn't possibly expect——'

'Alexandra would love to have another animal about the place.' He smiled slowly. 'And he would be quite safe. The house is situated on the outskirts of London in its own grounds of five acres overlooking farmland.'

Alexandra? He seriously thought she would give her Marmalade over to his *wife*?

'Alexandra is my daughter.' She knew instantly that he had read her mind again. The knowledge was there in the steely darkness of his eyes and the hard line of his mouth. 'Her mother and I were divorced four years ago, six months after Dee was born.'

'Oh.' She was totally out of her depth and it showed.

'Dee loves animals. She has a young cat of her own. I think Tabitha is about six months old now, and there are a couple of dogs about the place along with a few geese and hens and the usual tame hedgehogs and so on.'

'Oh.' It was weak, but all she could get past the blockage in her mind. Logan Steer as a family man? Never. And his wife? What on earth had happened with his wife? And why did he have custody of their daughter, if she had read their conversation correctly?

'That's settled, then.' He surveyed her through narrowed eyes.

'It is?' She was immensely glad the waiter chose that moment to bring their first course to the table, because at that precise moment she couldn't have argued any further. Something was hurting, deep inside, the pain almost as fierce as in the miserable days after their first encounter. *But she was over all that now*. Her mind spun dizzingly. She had been for years. So why was she feeling like this?

As the waiter left she stared down at her plate determinedly. She really had to pull herself together! This wasn't like her, it really wasn't.

'You can eat it, you know.' She came out of her reverie to find Logan watching her quietly, a twist of a smile pulling at his hard mouth. 'It tastes good.'

'I'm sure it does,' she answered primly as she glanced down at the small oval dish in front of her layered with strips of chicken breast, bacon, tomatoes and mushrooms on a highly seasoned bed of green salad, that went under the exotic name of Orient Melody. 'It looks delicious.'

'Doesn't it?' he agreed seriously, but she had seen the dark amusement shadowing his eyes and her temper flared hotly. He thought he was so in control of all this, of her—how she'd love to dent that monstrous ego just a tiny bit. '*Bon appetit.*'

She had to admit that the food was everything she had heard it would be. As course after course melted in her mouth accompanied by three different wines, all equally good, she found herself relaxing and responding to Logan's efforts to be the perfect host. It was as she smiled at another of his dry witty comments that a strange feeling began to steal over her, compounded of foreboding, unease and a disquietude that caught at her nerve-ends. She tried to capture what was wrong, but the good food and wine had dulled the edge of her perception. And then it came to her. She had felt as alive as this once before, just once, and then, as now, she had been tuned in perfectly to someone else's wavelength. Then she had felt warm, vital, interesting, with every nerve and emotion trembling and expectant, and it had ended in a disaster of unprecedented proportions. How could she have forgotten? Let down her guard just an iota? He hadn't changed. He had played her like a master musician that night eight years ago and he was doing the same now. And she had nearly fallen for it again.

She lowered her head and took a sip of wine. What was it about this man that cut through her defences so easily? And why did she dislike him so? She had a forgiving nature, too forgiving often, but when applied to Logan that divine attribute was quite absent. Everything about him grated on her but she didn't understand *why*. She frowned darkly.

'You really are the most difficult female to please. Is it me or the food?'

'What?' She raised her head sharply and met the narrowed blue eyes that were dark with an emotion that cleared instantly she caught his gaze.

'You still do it,' he said slowly, 'eight years later.'

'Do what?'

'Make me repeat everything I say.' He smiled with icy humour. She wished he wouldn't refer to their first meeting. When things were kept strictly in the present she could cope— just. But it was getting more difficult by the minute.

'Look, Logan, I want our relationship to be purely on a business level,' she said tightly as she met the blue eyes steadily.

'But of course.' He leant back in his chair and stretched lazily, his face enigmatic and closed. 'I wasn't aware I was suggesting anything else?'

'No, well, maybe not...' She found herself stammering and could have hit him for the way he made her feel, as though *she* had been propositioning *him*. And did he have to look so darkly attractive? she asked herself angrily. The sexual aura that was radiating off the big male body opposite should be canned and sold in the shops, she thought irritably. It'd make him a millionaire in a week.

'But now you mention it——' he eyed her wickedly '—all work and no play can be very boring.'

'Boring suits me just fine,' she answered grimly without the trace of a smile, stiffening as he straightened and leaned forward, his blue eyes stroking over her hot cheeks slowly before his gaze continued over to her mouth where it lingered for a painfully long moment.

'And Paul?' His eyes were suddenly a sharp silver and deadly serious. 'Does he fit into the nice little boring mould you seem to like so much?'

'I wasn't talking about Paul and you know it,' she answered angrily.

'Maybe not.' He didn't even seem to notice her fury. 'But somehow I can't quite believe that you are head over heels in love with young Hopkins, Melly.' The soft sarcasm made her ache to hit him. 'And you've got an untouched look about you, did you know that? I thought at first it was cultivated, a façade—you women seem to go in for an air of mystery, don't you?—but it's not. It's genuine. And very sexy.'

She glared at him, almost incoherent with rage. 'You are the most insufferable man I've ever met,' she said unsteadily as sheer anger made her voice shake.

'Why?' He eyed her lazily. 'Because I tell the truth? Most women would have taken what I've just said as an enormous compliment.'

'Well, I'm not most women,' she hissed furiously, 'although I've no doubt I'm talking to the leading expert on the subject.'

'Ow.' His amusement was incredibly infuriating in the circumstances. 'Those claws can still fetch blood. And why are you so mad? Because I'm right? How many men have you had, little Amelia Higginbottom? One, two? They certainly haven't touched that inner core, anyway.'

'I don't believe we are having this conversation.' She drank a glassful of wine straight down to try and cool the rage that had turned the blood in her veins to molten lava. 'How you can be so insensitive——?'

'Oh, I see.' He took a long sip of wine himself. 'You are allowed to cast aspersions on my sex life to your heart's content but I'm not allowed any questions regarding yours? I hardly think that's fair.'

'I don't care what you think is fair,' she said tightly, 'but not everyone has to leap in and out of bed like performing seals.'

'An interesting analogy,' he began lazily with mocking humour, only to stop abruptly as he met her eyes. 'You're not——' he stopped again as he sat upright in his seat, sheer amazement turning the silver-blue eyes almost transparent '—you can't be,' he said dazedly as his eyes ran over her hot face. 'Not in this day and age and not looking like you do. A virgin?'

'You can think exactly what you like.' She stood up with a composure she was far from feeling. 'And I'm going to powder my nose.'

She was aware of his eyes burning into the back of her head as she made her way to the ladies' cloakroom, but by the time she had daubed ice-cold water on her wrists and done a few very necessary breathing exercises into the mirror, the face looking back at her had lost the scarlet glow it had come in with. How dared he? She shut her eyes for a moment as the anger erupted again. Just who did he think he was anyway? The man was unbelievable.

As she made her way back to the table she saw he was leaning back in his chair looking up at the waiter as he talked, and for a second her heart stopped and then raced on like an express train. The big lean body was powerfully sensual and those devastatingly male good looks really were quite lethal. His ego must be jumbo-size. No doubt the women fell over themselves to make an impression on him.

She slipped into her seat, her thoughts making her lip curl slightly, to meet the full force of the ice-blue gaze.

'When are you bringing the cat to meet its peers?' he asked blandly, and she stared at him dumbly for a moment, nonplussed by the complete change of conversation.

'Marmalade isn't your problem,' she said grimly.

'No, but you will be if you aren't totally on the ball in Paris,' he said smoothly. 'You'll be doubling as secretary to me when needed, you know, and I want your mind firmly and completely on the job in hand, not worrying about some feline problem back in England.'

'Secretary to you?' This was the first she had heard of it and it showed. 'Who said that? There is no way——'

'That red hair has a lot to answer for.' His voice was cold now with disapproval. 'Are you always so unpleasant?' He held up an authoritative hand as she went to reply. 'Don't bother, I'll draw my own conclusions. You *will* help me out when needed, Melly, and you'll do it with courtesy and politeness. OK?' The blue eyes resembled polished glass now. 'Either that or you can tell Giles in the morning that the Paris deal is no go, at which point I would suspect you'll be looking for new employment.'

She stared at him angrily as he leant back in his seat as the waiter placed two large portions of a sticky chocolate and orange mousse, liberally laced with brandy and covered with thick fresh cream, in front of them.

'I see.' Her voice was taut with loathing when they were alone again. 'It seems I have no choice, then.'

'And the offer stands regarding the cat,' he said urbanely, ignoring the sparks shooting out of her eyes with lazy disregard. 'I would suggest you take me up on it if you care for the animal as you seem to. It would seem prudent to put his welfare before your own prejudices for once.'

'I always put Marmalade first,' she objected furiously, enraged at the suggestion that she was being unfair to the cat.

'Good. That's settled, then.' He lifted a silver spoon and dug into the rich dessert with every appearance of enjoyment. 'This is really very good.'

She glared at him without answering. The Logan of eight years ago was a little lamb compared to this swine. She was so angry she barely tasted the pudding at all. But if he thought he was going to have it all his own way he was very much mistaken! She wielded the spoon savagely as her thoughts sped on. OK, Logan Steer, so you want to play your little power games and convince yourself that you're still the best thing on two legs, she thought silently as she glanced at him over the crystal glasses and fine tableware. Well, that's fine by me, just fine. If you want war, that's exactly what you've got.

But this is one female who will walk away from you without a backward glance and with body and mind untouched. And *that*—her gaze at the handsome dark face opposite her became lethal—I promise you.

# CHAPTER THREE

As MELLY sat by Logan's side in his long, sleek, powerful Lamborghini with the cat-basket on her lap and Marmalade howling plaintively in time to every second that ticked by, her initial resolution that she was going to be the original ice-maiden was fast losing ground.

'Does it have to make that row?' Logan flashed a glance of pure irritation at the shaking wickerwork. 'And at such a pitch?'

'He's frightened.' Melly was finding the pitch he mentioned a little hard to take herself. Marmalade clearly wasn't prepared to suffer in silence. And she couldn't blame him really. One minute he had been snoozing in his nice warm basket after a huge dinner, without a care in the world, the next he had been whisked up and imprisoned in an unfriendly little tomb and carted in undignified protest into something that roared alarmingly and then proceeded to shake him consistently without so much as a by-your-leave. 'And he doesn't like it in the car.'

'*He* doesn't like it in the car?' Logan winced as a particularly shrill miaow tore through the car with enough power to make the eyeballs rattle. 'Is he going to keep that up all the way?'

'I've no idea,' Melly said tartly, 'and this was your suggestion, remember.'

'I do.' He groaned softly. 'Believe me, I do.' He switched on the radio but, after a few minutes of

Marmalade competing with the local pop station he declared Marmalade the winner and switched it off again.

'You're going to have to let him out of there,' Logan said a couple of miles later. Melly had noticed his knuckles were white as he gripped the steering-wheel but any satisfaction that she might have felt at seeing him totally at a loss was quelled by the pounding in her head. 'He might be quiet if he's free.'

'But your car?' She glanced over the immaculate upholstery of the beautiful car in trepidation. 'What if he...?' She stopped abruptly. 'Acts anti-socially?' she finished grimly.

'There is nothing more anti-social than that racket,' Logan said weakly, 'and frankly if he wants to go he'll have to go. In fact he can do anything short of driving this damn thing himself if he'll only keep his mouth shut. We've another twenty or so miles, Melly. Can *you* stand it?'

She held his glance for one split-second and then opened the top of the basket warily. Marmalade shot out like a jet-propelled missile, causing Logan to swear profusely, and landed in the back seat, spitting hellfire. But the howling had stopped. They drove another mile or so, hardly daring to breathe, and then Melly glanced round carefully. Marmalade gazed back at her, his huge green eyes reproachful, from his position on the back seat, and then stretched comfortably before curling up in a ginger ball and shutting his eyes.

'Well, that's put you and me in our places and established who's boss,' Logan said wryly. 'You weren't joking about the mind of his own, were you?' He glanced at her fleetingly. 'What did you do to acquire him? Put an advert in the paper asking for a feline extension of yourself? Only the most awkward applicants need apply?'

'Very funny.' Her glare didn't hold quite so much rage as she would have liked mainly because, with the howling having stopped, she had become painfully aware of the proximity of his big male body in the powerful expensive car, the Lamborghini being an aphrodisiac in itself. She hadn't wanted to drive down with him, she had *told* him that. She could have easily driven herself in the smart little Metro she had bought the year before. But he had swept all her objections aside and after the last two days of sheer chaos in the office she hadn't had the energy to argue with him. He shifted in his seat slightly, the movement flexing the muscles in his strong hard shoulders, and she felt an immediate ache in her lower stomach that annoyed her still further.

She glanced out of the window into the warm sunny September evening. They had left London behind and were on the outskirts now, where the harsh city streets had given way to gracious avenues and elegant cottages in their own grounds.

How could one man create such a volume of work, anyway? She thought back over the last week that had got worse each day once Logan had reappeared from his brief trip to France, the last two days culminating in an avalanche of work that had been impossible to finish. Giles had acquired a junior from the typing pool to help her, but the girl had been worse than useless once she had set eyes on Logan. He had seemed to transport the slim blonde into a helpless trance most of the time, and the fact that he had appeared merely irritated and then downright annoyed at her obvious enchantment had reduced the poor girl to a weeping mess by the end of the week.

'Dee is looking forward to meeting you.' She glanced up quickly and then took a little hard breath as her eyes locked briefly with his. This magnetism, sexual attraction, call it what you would, he had too much of the damn stuff! She found her senses racing as the faint scent of him teased her nostrils. It wasn't that he gave the impression of being a heavy macho man, she thought weakly as she nodded her reply to the handsome profile, his eyes now firmly concentrated on the road ahead, but there was something about him, something fascinating and arousing and all male, that made her more aware of herself as a woman than she would have dreamt possible. And Paul had sensed that.

She shut her eyes as she leant back against the beautiful leather. Over the last few days Paul's attitude had got distinctly proprietorial and it had nearly driven her mad. For the first time in their six-month relationship he had wanted to touch her all the time, hold her hand, meet her for lunch ... She shifted restlessly in her seat. And she had hated it. She hadn't liked the physical contact at all. Maybe she was frigid? She opened her eyes wide at the thought. Certainly after that one consuming encounter with Logan at the age of nineteen she had kept all further relationships with the opposite sex on a very definite platonic level. But she had set her sights on a career and put all her energies into that. Or had she been frightened? the little voice in her mind asked quietly. Frightened of losing control again, of being swept along on a tide of emotion that was unstoppable, of being nothing more than another man's plaything? *No*! For a moment her thoughts were so loud she thought Logan had heard them, but the cool profile was quite expressionless as she glanced his way. It hadn't been that, of course it hadn't.

She wanted, suddenly, to ask Logan a host of questions. About his wife, his daughter, his home. Did his ex see their daughter? Were they all still friends? And Logan, was he a good father? Or a resentful one, annoyed at being left with a child while his wife was as free as a bird?

The last question was answered within minutes of drawing up at the beautiful old house set in its acres of woodland on the edge of green sweeping fields full of grazing animals, the huge grounds making it totally private and secluded.

'Daddee!' As the car drew to a halt the shriek of welcome was plain to hear but, strangely, the small child sitting on the huge sweep of velvet-smooth lawn on an old rug covered with toys and books didn't rush to greet them. Rather it was Logan who covered the distance in two seconds and whisked the slight little form up high into his arms.

As Melly walked across to join them she felt a moment's ridiculous pain as Logan's daughter stared at her from enormous liquid brown eyes. She didn't look at all like her handsome father; in fact Melly couldn't see anything of Logan in the slim brown-haired child who stared at her so seriously. The small body was very thin and under-developed—in fact she hardly looked three years of age, let alone nearly five—but there was a vulnerability, a touching frailty in the tiny form, that made Melly want to reach out and hold her close. Instead she smiled warmly and spoke directly to the child, her eyes open and friendly. 'I hear you've offered to look after my cat for me? That's really very good of you, Alexandra. I was very worried about him.'

The large eyes continued their inspection for one more long moment before the whole body seemed to relax in

Logan's hold. 'I'm called Dee.' A quick grin flashed across the elfin face. 'When I like someone I let them call me that. Where's your cat? Can I see him?'

'Sure.' A warm glow at the little girl's immediate acceptance of her put a spring in Melly's steps as she hurried back to the car. Behave, Marmalade, behave, she cautioned the cat silently as she saw him sitting regally in the back seat contemplating his surroundings through the open window with a definite disdainful air about him. He could be difficult. Goodness knew he could be difficult! He was an animal of distinct prejudices and the last hour had not been to his liking.

'I told the housekeeper to keep the dogs out of the way this evening,' Logan said just behind her, 'until he's used to where he is.'

'Thank you...' As she turned, with her hand on the door, she felt the shock run in a little shiver the whole length of her spine but mercifully, somehow, she kept all trace from showing on her face.

Alexandra wasn't in her father's arms now. She was in a small wheelchair behind which Logan was standing, and although the child's big eyes were fixed eagerly on the large cat just visible through the open car window, Logan's gaze was tight on her face.

'Can you get him out? Does he scratch?' Alexandra was quite oblivious to any undercurrents as she held out thin little arms towards Marmalade. 'Can I hold him?'

'He doesn't usually scratch,' Melly said gently as she forced herself to concentrate totally on the matter in hand. 'But he's a bit frightened at the moment, I expect, so I'm not sure.'

The glance that Marmalade gave this announcement was one of pure narrow-minded contempt, and after one disgusted stretch he jumped out of the car and padded across to the wheelchair, winding his ginger body once round the wheels before peering up at Alexandra's enraptured face.

'He likes me.' The little girl twisted in the chair with satisfaction. 'Come on, come up here, Marmalade.' She tapped her lap invitingly. 'I want to say hello to you properly.' Perfectly on cue the big cat obeyed instantly, jumping up carefully into the small lap and rubbing against the thin chest before settling himself down with a swift kneading of his paws.

'Good grief!' Melly's astonishment was completely natural and therefore all the more gratifying to the brown eyes watching her from the chair. 'I've never known him to do that before.'

'Daddy says I have a way with animals.' Dee looked up at her gravely. 'Do you think so?'

'I know so!' Melly knelt down until she was on the same level as the child and smiled warmly into the small face. 'I can't think of anyone I'd rather leave Marmalade with and that's the truth, Dee. He loves you already.'

'Daddy says they know I won't hurt them,' the childish voice continued softly, 'because I don't run and shout and frighten them. He says that when we have something taken away from us there's always something better given if we look hard enough to find it.'

'I couldn't agree more.' Melly kept her eyes strictly on the child's earnest face. She had a feeling that a lot of Alexandra's conversation would begin with 'Daddy says', and the wisdom behind Logan's dealing with his daughter had caused a lump in her throat that was physically painful. 'You'll take care of him for me for a few weeks, then? Give him lots of cuddles as well as his food?'

'Yep.' The small face was very determined. 'And Tabitha will like having someone to play with. She gets bored sometimes with the dogs.'

'Does she?' Melly said a quick mental prayer. Marmalade's track record with the rest of the feline species wasn't particularly glowing and the dog population in the neighbouring gardens held him with both respect and fear.

'Can I show him to the others?' Alexandra twisted round in the chair to look up at Logan who had been quite silent throughout the whole exchange. 'Now?'

'I guess so.' Logan's quizzical gaze revealed that his thoughts were along the same lines as hers, Melly thought dismally. 'But don't be worried if they take a little time to be friends.'

'They won't.' Alexandra looked down at the big cat still sitting in apparently relaxed ease on her lap. 'I've told the others he's coming and now I'll tell him to be good. You will be good, won't you, Marmalade? No fighting or hissing or anything? Tabitha wants to meet you and so do Patch and Whisky. They won't hurt you and you've got to behave.' Marmalade's huge green eyes blinked sleepily at the small face and for a moment Melly could have sworn the big tom-cat nodded.

The rest of the evening passed in something of a dreamlike state. Marmalade had been forbearance itself when meeting his peers, allowing himself just one swift swipe with a sheathed paw when one of the dogs was a little too inquisitive, after which, point made, he allowed the other animals the usual inspection of certain parts of his anatomy with unusual good grace.

Melly had spent another hour with Alexandra before the child was carried up to bed by the stout little housekeeper, during which time she found Logan's daughter both delightful and charming. Logan had kept pretty much in the background, pleading paperwork he had to clear before dinner, although she had felt the excuse didn't ring quite true. There had been something... Something veiled and hidden behind the ice-blue eyes that she couldn't quite read. But he clearly adored the small child and Alexandra idolised him, almost every sentence beginning with the inevitable 'Daddy says'. She didn't mention her mother once during the evening and, although Melly was burning with curiosity, neither did she. She had noticed in one corner of the huge drawing-room on a small occasional table a photograph of Logan holding a very tiny baby in his arms while a beautifully dressed slim blonde gave a strained smile into the camera, but hadn't liked to ask the child any questions. It would have been insensitive, clumsy, and so she had kept the conversation very general.

'Ready for dinner?' Logan smiled at her as he walked back into the drawing-room after disappearing upstairs to kiss Alexandra goodnight. 'I'm starving.'

She stared at him silently. He had originally tried to persuade her to stay overnight, using the excuse that they were travelling to Paris on the same flight the next morning as his reason, but she had side-stepped that plan with immense firmness, declaring that her absence would be a good chance to see how Marmalade settled down without her. If he didn't adjust to his new surroundings she didn't know what she would do, but it would seem that worry was taken care of anyway. At the present moment he was lying with an adoring Tabitha pressed into his side in front of the crackling log fire the house-keeper had lit a few minutes before, the very epitome of the cat with everything. But now she intended to ask

Logan the question that had been burning on her tongue ever since she had seen Alexandra.

'Why didn't you tell me?' She looked him straight in the eyes as she spoke, her gaze steady. 'Wouldn't it have been better for me to be prepared in case I had said something wrong?'

He didn't try to pretend he didn't understand, holding her eyes for a long moment before turning to walk across to the well stocked drinks cabinet at the side of the huge old mantelpiece. 'Sherry, a glass of wine, before dinner?' He indicated the array of bottles with a wave of his hand. 'Or something else maybe?'

'Sherry would be fine.' She waited until he had poured the drink and then asked him again. 'Why, Logan?'

He handed her the drink unsmilingly and then shrugged big powerful shoulders slowly. He had changed out of the suit he had been wearing at the office, and the casual black silk shirt and jeans he now wore made him seem younger somehow and devastatingly attractive. She stiffened slightly as the thought took form. Careful, Melly, careful, she told herself silently, remember where that physical fascination got you before.

'I wanted you to see her as she is,' he said quietly after a full minute had ticked by in complete silence, 'with no pre-conceived ideas about her handicap. Too often people think the brain is affected as well as the body in such circumstances and I didn't want...' He stopped abruptly. 'I don't know what I wanted,' he finished softly. 'Just for you to see her as she is.'

'She's beautiful,' Melly said quietly as she thought of the engaging little face under its cap of sleek brown hair, 'and very bright.'

'Yes, she is.' He stared at her for a long moment before moving to her side with that lethal cat-like walk of his that always brought the image of a wild animal into the screen of her mind. 'Beautiful and very courageous.'

As he bent his head and took her lips she stood very still, her eyes wide open, as she nerved her body to remain motionless. The kiss was very brief, hardly a caress at all, but for minutes afterwards her lips burnt as though they had been brushed with fire.

'There were several problems that became apparent after she was born,' he continued as though the kiss had never been, walking across to a large easy chair just behind the cats and indicating the one opposite to her. She sank into it gingerly. Things were suddenly too intimate. The cosy drink before dinner, the cats curled up in front of the fire, the two chairs snugly placed . . . This was Logan, for goodness' sake. *Logan*. She forgot that at her peril. 'A malformation of the spinal column, the kidneys weren't working properly and, most seriously of all, a hole in the heart.' He didn't look at her as he spoke but as she glanced across at his face she saw it was dark with pain. 'The last two difficulties have been overcome—she had an operation on her heart last year— but it will take some time to catch up on lost growth.'

'And her back?' she asked softly.

He turned to look at her, his eyes cloudy, and suddenly she would have given the world to be able to reach out to him and take away the grief that had turned the blue eyes silver-grey. 'Maybe.' He shook his head slowly. 'There's an operation scheduled for the end of the year. The doctors couldn't do it before because she was too weak. But I don't know.' Suddenly the dynamic ruthless businessman had vanished and the worried father that remained caused her heart to pound so frantically she thought for a moment she would faint. 'It's a fifty-fifty chance—perhaps I shouldn't put her through it.'

She heard him, and the enormity of the problem caught at her heart like a knife, but the main emotion she felt at that split second of time was sheer horror at her reaction to his pain. She didn't *want* to care about this man, she didn't *want* to get involved, however ephemerally, in his private life, she didn't dare.

Her mind was racing, but through the sick churning she caught on to that one thought and held on. She didn't dare. She wouldn't analyse why. She just knew she didn't dare.

'What does her mother think about the operation?' She heard her voice speaking the words almost coolly and marvelled that her vocal cords could be so controlled when the rest of her was such a mess. 'I presume you've asked her opinion?'

He seemed to stiffen infinitesimally but then, as the face he turned to her was bland and urbane, she decided she must have imagined it. 'Of course.' He nodded slowly. 'But Vanessa leaves those sorts of decisions to me. She finds it difficult to cope with illness in any form.'

'I see.' What a stupid thing to say, she thought angrily; you don't see at all!

'That was one of the reasons we decided to divorce,' he continued carefully. 'We didn't see eye to eye on the problems facing Dee. Vanessa felt...' He stopped abruptly. 'She didn't quite understand the medical complexity,' he finished smoothly, and somehow she knew the conversation was at an end.

How could a mother leave her sick baby like that? She took a quick gulp of sherry to calm the nausea. And did he condone it? Did he still love her? He certainly hadn't condemned her anyway. 'You're still in contact?' she asked flatly through stiff lips.

'Yes.' He rose and walked across to the large full-length windows to stand with his back to her as he looked out on to the floodlit garden beyond, a row of silver birches at the end of the green lawn turning the scene into one of fairy-tale beauty. 'She is Alexandra's mother.'

And your ex-wife, she thought painfully and, if that photograph is anything to go by, extremely beautiful. Was he hoping they would get back together again? She took a deep breath to calm the fluttering in her chest. Obviously it would be wonderful for the child to have her parents reunited. And Logan? Did he think it would be wonderful?

'Dinner's ready, Mr Steer.' The soft Somerset drawl of the housekeeper cut into the silence that had fallen on the room and Melly turned to her with a smile of almost desperate relief on her face. She wanted to get out of this. Oh, she did, so much.

She tried, very hard, to respond normally to Logan's conversation through dinner but could hear her voice making the necessary rejoinders even as her mind operated on quite a different plane altogether.

Part of her was with the small child sleeping upstairs who still had so much to face in her young life. Part of her kept seeing Logan's face as he spoke of his daughter's problems and the other part, the main part, was dissecting all the information her mind had absorbed and searching for an answer to... An answer to what? she asked herself flatly as her heart pounded. There wasn't even a question that she was aware of.

She had never felt so confused and upset and helplessly bewildered in her life. Not even eight years ago. She should never have come to his home with him like this; it had altered things somehow and caused a hundred

jabbing questions in her mind that she wasn't prepared
even to acknowledge. She should have been stronger.
Blow Paris. Blow the job. Blow even Marmalade. *She
should never have come*.

# CHAPTER FOUR

'OK?' As Logan's quiet voice brought her eyes snapping from the mass of brilliantly white cotton-wool clouds visible through the small plane window, she nodded stiffly.

'Fine, thank you.' She had been trying, very hard, to ignore the effect the big male body seated in the seat next to her was having on her nervous system, and now she managed a tight smile as she met the narrowed blue eyes. 'I love flying.'

'Yes, I thought you would.' The deep voice was almost expressionless. 'You see it as a magical world out there? Where cherubim might pop up behind a drifting cloud or slide on sunbeams in a sea of blue?'

'How did you know?' The words were out before she had thought and she bit her lip hard as she met the amused silver-blue eyes that moved over her hot face slowly.

'Oh, Melly...' He shook his head slowly, and suddenly all the amusement had gone and there was something, something unbearably warm melting the ice-cool gaze. 'Don't ever change. I still can't believe now you're real.'

As their gaze caught and held she felt herself shiver, as much with panic as anything else, and forced her eyes away from his with an almost physical jolt. Charm. He was loaded with the stuff and it didn't mean a thing. She would be the biggest fool on earth if she let herself think for one moment that it did. 'You go in for in-

furiating women, then?' she asked quietly with just the
right amount of mocking amusement to turn their conversation into nothing more than social repartee. 'With
a mind of their own? Awkward?'

He acknowledged all his earlier comments on her
character with a rueful nod of his head as that devastating smile flashed briefly across the hard face. 'If they
have hair the colour of a dying sunset and brown eyes
a man could drown in,' he said softly, the words a caress
in themselves.

She forced an answering smile on to her face with sheer
will-power. 'Or if they are slim and blonde or dark and
voluptuous?' she smiled sweetly. 'How sensible of you,
Logan.'

He eyed her darkly for one long moment before relaxing back into his seat with a deep frown wrinkling
his brow. 'One day, Amelia Higginbottom,' he muttered
grimly, 'one day...'

'One day what?' She wasn't sure why but suddenly
she felt unusually aggressive, and more with herself than
him. How could she be so darn pathetic as to respond,
even for a moment, to that synthetic charm of his? And
she had. She almost groaned out loud. That treacherous
warmth in her lower stomach and fluttery feeling in her
throat wouldn't be denied.

'One day I shall have your body beneath mine again.'
He had shut his eyes and the low voice was barely
audible. 'But this time there'll be no knock at the door,
no reprieve. You will be mine, *completely*, tamed and
obedient and on fire for what only I can give you.' As
the soft voice stopped speaking she found herself staring
at the dark face dazedly as she struggled to take in what
he had just said, doubting her own ears. 'I thought that

would shut you up.' The quiet voice was ripe with satisfaction.

'You arrogant, conceited——'

'Shush, sweetheart, shush...' The silver-blue eyes opened and held her furious brown ones as he placed a warning finger on her lips. 'You don't want the esteemed Mr Trent or his minions to hear our love-talk, do you?'

'Love-talk?' She ground out the words through clenched teeth as he laughed mockingly. 'From a swine like you? You don't know the meaning of the word "love", Logan, only in the basest four-letter sense. I'd sooner walk naked through London than ever willingly let you touch me again.'

'The lady doth protest too much, methinks.' The piercing eyes ran slowly over her angry face and continued a slow inspection of her body through half-closed lids. 'But the walk through London is something to think about. Unlike you, I find travelling more than a little tedious, but with that delightful vision at the back of my mind...'

She glared at him angrily and he smiled slowly before settling lazily in his seat again and shutting his eyes. 'And say what you like, my red-haired vixen, you can't deny there's something between us.'

'I certainly can.' She stared at the relaxed form next to her as sheer frustration made her voice tremble. 'I loathe you, Logan, you might as well know it——'

'No, you don't.' He interrupted her low shaking voice without opening his eyes. 'You might think you do, but you don't.'

'And if the expert on women says it, it must be true?' she asked bitterly.

'Exactly.' Now his eyes did open for the barest of moments and she saw they were an icy silver, cool and distant. 'And don't push your luck too far, Melly. I've been very patient and understanding so far—I felt I owed you that for the misunderstanding in the past—but my magnanimity can be exhausted, so take care.'

'Misunderstanding?' Her voice emerged in a shrill shriek and as Giles, seated a couple of rows in front of them and deep in conversation with Alfred Hynes, turned round with an enquiring lift of his eyebrows, she took a long hard pull of air before smiling and nodding at him as she deliberately ignored the question on his square face. 'There was no misunderstanding,' she said tightly, 'and as for your magnanimity, you know exactly where you can put that.'

'Charming.' The deep voice was mildly reproving and grated on her like barbed wire. 'Not exactly the tenor of conversation I would expect from Giles's personal secretary.'

'I'm not talking to you any more.' She tried to keep all defeat out of her voice as she turned away in her seat and stared determinedly out of the window again.

He didn't answer, the closed eyelids and relaxed body an answer in themselves. This was just a game to him. She glanced at the silent figure before turning away again. An amusing pastime, a little diversion, an interesting duel of words with a sexual undertone that would appeal to his jaded palate. She hated him. She nodded bitterly to herself. *She did*.

And last night? Even as the question probed into her mind she felt herself stiffen with despair. She didn't want to think about last night but somehow her brain wouldn't acknowledge the fact.

After dinner they had sat and talked over coffee in the dimly lit drawing-room, the cats still snoozing in front of the fire and the two dogs sprawled some distance away twitching and grumbling in their sleep as though protesting at the feline domination of the warmth. It had been ... cosy, cosy and snug and infinitely appealing to her tired mind, and she had fought the feeling with all her might. She couldn't relax near Logan, not for a minute. There was something about the big male body and cool hooded eyes that kept her nerves as tight as coiled wires even without past history as a reminder to point out the real man.

He had been very correct and composed, his imperturbable face giving nothing away as he kept the conversation general and almost businesslike. He hadn't mentioned Vanessa again and, although part of her was relieved, there was a persistent burning curiosity nagging away at the back of her mind that was making her as jumpy as a cricket.

'That was lovely, but I must go now.' As the beautiful antique grandfather clock in one corner of the elegant room had chimed ten she had spoken nervously into the tight silence that had fallen on the room in the last few minutes, and he had risen instantly, his face closed and dark and his movements abrupt.

'Of course. I'll take you home.'

It had hurt quite ridiculously that Marmalade had made no effort to follow her as she had left the house and that emotion, compounded with all the others that had had her head whirling all evening, kept her body stiff and tight and her face taut as they had driven home. She felt Logan's eyes on her face once or twice but he hadn't spoken, for which she was supremely grateful.

She had never been so near bursting into tears in her life and the feeling horrified her.

'Here we are.' As the car glided to a halt outside her house she forced a bright, non-committal smile into place as her hand reached for the door-handle.

'Thank you very much for a lovely evening and for taking care of Marmalade,' she said quickly, 'and Dee is delightful. I think——'

He never did hear what she thought. One moment he had been sitting facing her, watching her as she spoke, his face a mass of conflicting shadows in the dark car, and the next he had pulled her violently into his arms, his mouth closing on hers in an agony of need that fired every single one of her senses and caused her heart to pound so hard she felt faint. Almost instantly the kiss softened, the demanding possessiveness of his mouth and tongue intoxicatingly sensual but non-threatening and shockingly familiar. She remembered how this felt! Eight years melted away in a second and she was plunged back into a raw awareness of what a man's touch, a man's mouth, could do to her body, *and she couldn't resist*. She couldn't even think.

As his mouth roamed over her face, pausing to nibble sensuously at her ear before continuing in a blindingly warm exploration of her throat, she heard herself moan slightly and the sound appalled her. And in the same moment she was free and the realisation that his arms were no longer holding her close almost made her moan again.

He had left the car and opened her door before she drew breath, his face a study in self-control. His very silence, the swiftness of events, had her climbing numbly out of the Lamborghini as his hand closed over her elbow, and before she knew what was happening she was in the house, the door had closed and the roar of a powerful engine in the dark street outside told her he had gone. Still without a word being exchanged.

She sank weakly on to the tiny stool in the small hall as her legs gave away, unable to believe the last few minutes had really taken place. But her bruised lips, the thudding of her heart and aching twist in the pit of her stomach told her differently. And she hadn't even tried to push him away! She groaned deep in her chest and dropped her head between her hands as she twisted on the upholstered wood. What would he be thinking now? She bit her lip until she tasted blood. That she was a pushover? That she was the type of woman who said one thing and meant another? That she wanted him?

She shivered in the darkness, the house unbearably empty without Marmalade's comforting presence. She didn't want him. Of course she didn't. He was the last man on earth... As the tears came in an overwhelming flood, she gave in to their salty heat with a little despairing cry, utterly forlorn. Why had he had to come back into her life like this? Everything had been wonderful, she had had everything she could possibly want...

Much later, as she had slipped into bed, utterly exhausted, her normal logic had risen above the panic and hurt. He had kissed her goodnight. Nothing more and nothing less. It had been stupid, *she* had been stupid to allow it, but a kiss was a kiss and nothing to get so het-up about. She nodded to herself in the darkness. Goodness, in the world that they both inhabited, social kissing was as ordinary as a casual handshake. It had meant nothing, less than nothing.

A social kiss? She ground her teeth together as the little voice intruded. Yes, a social kiss. That had been all it meant to a man like him. And all it meant to her.

She *wouldn't* allow it to mean more. But she would never let him kiss her like that again. She curled under the covers and dragged the pillow over her head in an effort to cut out further thought. Never ever again...

'Your seatbelt?' She came back to the present with a hard jolt as Logan's voice spoke directly into her ear, and raised her eyes to see a smiling stewardess nodding benevolently in the aisle. 'You have to fasten your seatbelt, Melly.'

'You were far away.' The beautifully made-up face was smiling at her but the huge green eyes had fastened on Logan in the next instant as he glanced her way, and they were frankly appreciative. 'Didn't hear a word I said.'

'I'll look after her.' Logan dismissed the stewardess with a warm smile, earning himself another smouldering glance in the process before the girl glided off to check the other passengers.

'I'm perfectly capable of looking after myself,' Melly snapped indignantly, furious at the patronising attitude.

'I don't doubt that for a minute.' Logan indicated her seatbelt again and she fastened it with jerky hands that anger made clumsy. 'But sooner or later we all need someone, Melly, even you. And it's nice to be cared for sometimes, take it from me.'

'And of course you'd know all about being cared for,' Melly said coldly, her reaction to the softness in his voice making her voice scathing. How could that note in his voice induce a quiver deep in her limbs when she *knew* what he was like? 'No doubt you're an authority on that, among other things.'

'Doesn't your mind ever rise above mere sex?' he asked lazily, his eyes wickedly amused as the flush that started on the high sweep of her cheekbones rapidly covered her whole face. 'You really do need taking in hand, my girl.'

'You are such a—such a ...' She was still searching for words as he laughed softly, taking her hand as it rested on the arm of the seat and imprisoning it within his, oblivious to her immediate protest.

'Now just relax and be a good girl while we land,' he said with mocking sternness. 'You don't want Giles to think we aren't friends, do you?'

The explicitness of the word she said in reply made the dark eyebrows rise fractionally as he shook his head slowly, his eyes rueful as they stroked over her hot face. 'Amelia Higginbottom, wherever did you learn such language? I'm ashamed of you.' Her glare of rage was so fierce that he laughed again, a slow deep chuckle of sheer enjoyment. 'And I was right, you do need taking in hand.'

She ignored him then, settling back in her seat and shutting her eyes as the plane circled for landing, her hand still trapped in his and her body stiff with outrage.

Once through Customs they found Giles, Alfred and the two industrial engineers that Giles had brought over for a few days waiting for them, Giles obviously champing at the bit. 'All ready, then?' He was striding towards the exit before anyone could answer, his small, stocky, square frame fairly bristling with frustrated energy, but once outside among the fleet of taxis Logan very firmly deposited her case and his in one as Giles's entourage claimed another.

'We'll see you at the hotel, Giles,' Logan said easily as he ushered Melly into the depths of the big vehicle and the last sight she had of Giles was his rather startled face as they drove away. Very few people had the nerve to take the initiative around Giles but then, she reasoned silently, lack of nerve was not an attribute she had reckoned to Logan.

'Have you been to Paris before?' Logan asked quietly as the vehicle entered the main stream of traffic to a crazy blaring of horns and with utter disregard for any form of highway code, as far as she could ascertain.

'Once.' She glanced at him carefully. 'Many years ago.'

'And did you like it?'

She shrugged slowly. 'I can't remember.'

'You can't remember?' He eyed her in amazement. 'Paris is not a city you can't remember. How old were you anyway?'

'Seven or eight.'

'That explains it.' She could just feel his thigh against hers on the seat and, although the pressure was so slight as to be unnoticeable, it was having the effect of hot fire which intensified as he placed a casual arm at the back of her shoulders and leant forward to wave an expansive hand at the view from the car window. 'It's the city of dreams, Melly.' His face was so close to hers as he gazed out of the window that if she moved an inch she could kiss the hard tanned jaw already shadowed with faint stubble, and as the thought materialised she had to force herself not to jerk away. 'Eternally romantic, richly cultural and with a magic all its own.' He turned to look down at her, the cool narrowed eyes vivid slits of blue in his dark face.

'You obviously approve.' She aimed to make her voice dry.

'So will you.' He smiled slowly. 'So will you, my prickly little vixen. If any city can melt that heart of stone, Paris can.'

'I have not got a heart of stone,' she began indignantly, only to stop as he placed a reproving finger on her lips.

'Be quiet. I want to show you some of the sights as an aperitif.'

And it was beautiful. As they drove to their Left Bank hotel through noisy crowded streets with the soaring spear of the Eiffel Tower making the skyline instantly recognisable, the sheer colour and life of the city reached out to enfold her in its spell. They passed old museums, countless statues seemingly at every street corner, intricately carved stone churches and an abundance of fountains and squares, and all bathed in the mild September sunshine that lit up the dusty bookstalls and bohemian restaurants in the Latin Quarter with fascinating charm. There seemed to be market stalls everywhere, brilliant splashes of colour spilling on to cobbled streets and modern pavements and causing even more chaos and noise.

As they passed the Sorbonne University in the Latin Quarter on the River Seine's smaller left bank, Logan pointed to the ancient building through the car window, moving his head slightly so that the warm male smell of him, reminiscent of lemon and aftershave and something intangible, caused her nerves to tighten in immediate response. 'The university has Roman origins dating back to 50 BC,' he said quietly as his clean breath stroked her cheek in a soft caress. 'This is the oldest part of Paris.'

'Is it?' She desperately wanted to move, to put some distance between herself and that powerful body that was causing her to go weak at the knees, but he seemed quite oblivious to their closeness, his eyes on the changing scene outside and his countenance unperturbed.

'We should reach our hotel soon. I told the driver to take the scenic route, so no doubt Giles and company are already waiting.' He smiled wryly. 'With a full day's work mapped out.' She nodded a silent reply as she steeled herself to sit perfectly still. The thought of work, good old-fashioned straightforward work, had never seemed so appealing. After a day of doing the job she did so well, maybe her mind would be her own again.

As they came to yet another unscheduled halt in the heavy stream of traffic she found her eyes drawn to a young couple sitting outside a small restaurant sipping coffee but with their eyes fastened on each other's faces. They couldn't have been more than twenty years of age, obviously students, the girl's hair long and shining down her back and with a sweet young face scrubbed clean of make-up, and the boy dark and rough-looking with clothes that had seen better days. But his expression wasn't rough as he stared at his sweetheart, the look on the young lad's face causing Melly's heart to jump into her mouth. The hands not holding the coffee-cups were entwined on the table, their bodies leant towards each other as though they couldn't bear to be apart for a moment, their whole demeanour making it clear they were blind and deaf to anything around them.

'Young love.' She hadn't been aware that Logan had followed her gaze but now, as she turned to the sound of his voice, she saw the blue eyes had been aware of her interest. 'Free of mortgages, financial commitment, nappies, all the entanglements the human race seem to enter into so willingly.'

'Did you?' The words were out before she knew she had even thought them.

'Enter into them willingly?' Suddenly the hard face was closed and cold, almost as though a mask had settled on the handsome features. 'I've got no complaints. I've got Dee, after all.'

'Yes.' She turned back to the young couple who were still immersed in each other's eyes. He had Dee, and Dee's mother? The child provided a link with Vanessa that was forged in steel. They had created new life between them, shared moments of intimacy that meant more than just a night's casual passion. He had *married* her, for goodness' sake. Did he still love her? She remembered that beautiful face in the photograph and felt sick. Of course he did. It was obvious who had walked out on whom. Vanessa had left him and he wanted her back. That was why he kept all the avenues of communication open through their daughter.

As the traffic moved on, Melly stared unseeing out of the window, her eyes cloudy with thoughts. The rue Mouffetard was busy and crowded although still managing to retain much of its medieval atmosphere, packed as it was with restaurants, pavement cafés and shops, but Melly was blind and deaf to the colourful scene outside the car.

Passion and love, even to the extreme, were very much a part of Paris's magic, and she forgot that at her peril. This scintillating capital was tailor-made for a man like Logan. Even the very air was soft with romance and seduction. She had to be careful, very careful.

As though to confirm her thoughts Logan moved slightly beside her, taking her chin in his hand and turning her face to look into his. '*Pour être Parisien, il n'est pas nécessaire d'être né à Paris; il suffit d'y renaître,*' he said softly, his voice low and deep. 'To be a Parisian one need not be born in Paris, only reborn there. It's an old French proverb,' he added quietly as her wide brown eyes stared into the hard blue of his.

'Perhaps I don't want to be a Parisian,' Melly said slowly as she forced her voice to betray none of her inner agitation. 'Perhaps I'm happy to be just English.'

'Perhaps.' Logan's face was still and quiet. 'Or is it that you are frightened of life, Melly? Scared to take a chance on something that isn't completely in your control? Do you want to stay a career woman, marry someone like Paul and have two point five children and a comfortable home with an *au pair* to see to the offspring?'

'Is that so wrong?' She jerked her face free of his fingers and leant back against the window as she faced him angrily.

'Not if it's what you really want,' he said quietly, 'but the Melly I see beneath that beautiful skin of yours isn't like that. There's fire there, fire and warmth and passion. That life would never satisfy you in the end. You would grow sad and bitter trapped in a little box of your own making, and Paul would suffer too. Without meaning to, you'd make his life hell.'

'Logan, you have no right to say all this.' She could feel her face was burning with colour but as usual he was cool and unruffled, a slightly quizzical expression turning the blue eyes silver. 'It's absolutely none of your business what I do with my life. And I love Paul.' She didn't know why she added that last sentence unless it was a talisman, a protection against the trembling warmth that had flooded her whole body. 'Our relationship——'

'Relationship?' Her declaration had turned his narrowed eyes icy cold, changing the handsome face into a severe mask. 'You don't call that tepid friendship a relationship in any sense, do you? And love?' His eyes glittered with arctic frost. 'You don't even know the

meaning of the word! Did you ache when you had to
leave him to come to Paris, long for his touch first thing
in the morning and last thing at night, sigh his name in
your dreams——?'

'How dare you?' Her voice was a low hiss now and
filled with hot anger. The contempt in his voice had been
biting. 'What gives you the right to think you can tell
me about love? You! Of all people!' She glared at him
furiously. 'You haven't got a clue——'

'We've arrived.' His voice was suddenly expressionless, his face bland, and as she stared at him
blankly and then paused to look out of the window she
saw they were outside a magnificent old building with
huge stone steps leading on to the old cobbled street.
'Our hotel. And I think that's Giles...'

As Giles strode down the steps to meet them Logan
stepped out of the taxi and moved round to open her
door, his stance stiffening very slightly as she ignored
his proffered hand and scrambled from the interior of
the vehicle with more haste than elegance. How dared
he interrogate her like this? His ego really was beyond
belief. To insinuate that poor Paul wasn't right for her!
As they all moved into the hotel, the men carrying the
cases between them, she found her mind was racing and
scarcely took in the luxurious opulence all around her.
Maybe Paul *wasn't* right for her. She found the thought
didn't have the power to dismay her at all, probably because it crystallised a feeling that had been growing for
days, weeks. But that was *her* business and not Logan's.
Besides which, a man like Logan couldn't understand
the easy affection she and Paul shared, a fondness that
had nothing to do with sex but everything to do with
respect and consideration and mutual regard! She glared
at Logan's back as he moved to the reception desk and

spoke to the slim chic French girl in charge. 'Tepid friendship.' Suddenly his words burnt hotly in her mind. It wasn't! Not really, not exactly... The denial was weak even to her own ears and renewed her outrage. Tepid friendship or not, it was her own affair and not Logan's!

The next few hours sped by in a whirl of hard work and new impressions that effectively stopped her mind from thinking about anything else but the job in hand. Giles had reserved a suite of rooms on the top floor of the hotel and she had to admit her boss had been more than generous in his choice of accommodation. Her own room had everything from air-conditioning, satellite TV, minibar and telephone to a huge *en-suite* bathroom marbled in dusky pink that made her feel like one of the large-eyed heroines from the silent screen.

A small room leading off her bedroom interconnected with Giles's and had been set out as a mini-office complete with bar, coffee-maker and a replica of her own word processor in England, along with a dozen other of the labour-saving gadgets that Giles loved so much. Logan's room was across the corridor, for which she was thankful. The thought of hearing him moving about, preparing for bed, sent a little shiver snaking down her spine.

Dinner was to be taken in the elegant gourmet restaurant in the hotel and Giles had arranged they all meet in the small cocktail lounge first for drinks before the meal. After typing a long report on one of the possible sites, Melly finished with minutes to spare and, pausing merely to shower the grime of the long day away before slipping into a little evening dress in dark blue velvet, she decided to do without make-up, running a comb through her thick curls before applying just a touch of mascara at the last minute to liven up the somewhat strained face in the mirror. She didn't want to go down-stairs and eat with Logan. She did't want to do any-thing with Logan—ever. Nevertheless, as the lift took her swiftly downwards she was honest enough to admit that the feeling bubbling in her chest was one of ex-citement and anticipation and her weakness made her doubly determined to be very cool, very distant and very reserved. She was going to have to avoid him, whenever and however she could.

'You look lovely.' As she joined the others seated at the long bar in the small glass room at one side of the restaurant, Logan pulled a stool out for her at his side, moving in such a way that his body effectively cut her off from the other men. 'I've taken the liberty of or-dering you the cocktail of the day. Is that all right?'

'Fine.' It wasn't. It implied an intimacy that wasn't theirs but she wasn't going to be small-minded enough to protest, and when the drink came it was delicious.

'Blue suits you.' He was all charm again tonight, she thought tightly, as she looked into the cool narrowed eyes, charm and lethal good looks. He was devastatingly assured in a beautifully cut black dinner jacket that en-hanced the big masculine shoulders while the matching trousers hugged the lean hips in a way guaranteed to catch even the most matronly eye.

'Black suits *you*.' She eyed him unsmilingly. 'But I'm sure you know that already.' She saw the careful insult register in the steel-blue of his eyes seconds before Giles moved his heavy square body round at the side of Logan and effectively drew them to join the others.

The dinner was delicious but she barely tasted a thing, eating each course mechanically as she joined in the polite conversation and laughed at all the right times while her whole being was concentrated on the cold watchful face across the table, aware of each piercing flick of the silver-blue eyes across her face even though she never glanced directly at him. He was angry. She knew that. And he was hiding it well, talking with the others and providing the kind of witty repartee that Giles loved even while his mind moved on quite a different plane altogether. But she didn't care. He *wasn't* going to have this all his own way. He had forced himself back in her life, taken hold of her senses, contrived that she come to this foreign country where she was completely at his mercy... She knew, even as she thought the accusations, that they weren't quite true, but they were true enough! She didn't trust him, she didn't like him and there was no way she was going to play his seduction game for a few weeks until he moved on to the next job and the next woman.

'Shall we retire to the lounge for coffee?' Giles asked pleasantly as the meal came to a close, rising and pulling back Melly's chair as he took her arm.

'Not for me, thanks.' Melly kept her eyes on Giles as she spoke but she was aware of Logan in the background as they all left the restaurant and, although he hadn't spoken, his silence said far more than mere words. 'I'm a bit tired, the travelling and everything. I think I'll go straight to bed if you don't mind.'

'Not at all.' Giles smiled genially, obviously well pleased with the day's progress, and after including the others in a general sweep of her head Melly walked quickly towards the lift, vitally conscious of a tall dark figure standing just a little apart from the others as he watched her disappear.

Once in her room she kicked off the blue velvet shoes she had bought with the dress and flexed her aching feet in the thick wool carpet. She was tired, she was confused and nothing was right. 'You need a good night's sleep, my girl,' she told the pale reflection in the dressing-table mirror. 'That's all that's wrong with you. You're in Paris, you're young, everything's wonderful.' The eyes that stared back at her were frankly disbelieving and she turned away in disgust, peeling off the dress and her undies before donning her thick short towelling robe preparatory to taking a shower.

The sharp knock at the door a second later almost made her jump out of her skin and she found herself clutching her throat nervously before she brought her hand down abruptly with an exclamation of self-disgust. 'You're as nervous as a kitten,' she told herself quietly as she walked slowly towards the door. 'For goodness' sake, pull yourself together. They'll be taking you back to England in a straitjacket if you carry on like this.'

'Hello again.' As she opened the door Logan detached himself from the wall opposite where he had been leaning and moved into the doorway, his big body seeming to fill the small space. 'I've just rung England and thought I'd let you know how the boss is doing.'

'The boss?' She stared at him vacantly as her nerves went haywire. His bow tie was undone and hanging round his shirt collar, and the first few open inches of the white silk shirt exposed enough dark curling body hair to turn her legs to liquid and the pit of her stomach to molten lava.

'Marmalade.' He indicated the room beyond her with a lazy wave of his hand. 'Can I come in for a minute?'

As she searched desperately for a plausible reason to say no she found herself nodding dazedly and, as he brushed past her into the room beyond, the casual touch of his body as he passed and the sensual delicious smell of him caused sheer panic to grip her throat.

She'd done it again! Fallen in with a suggestion of his as though she were a seven-year-old instead of twenty-seven! What was the matter with her when she was around him? And he was dangerous. As she turned to face him she saw the dark features were quiet and still, the blue eyes watching her intently as she moved back into the room. Yes, he was dangerous, very dangerous and never more so than when he was cool and watchful as now.

# CHAPTER FIVE

'WOULD you like to sit down?' She indicated a big easy-chair just behind him with a wave of her hand, painfully conscious of the length of bare leg the short robe exposed and vitally aware of her nakedness under the thick towelling.

Logan, on the other hand, was his usual lazy, sardonic self, seating himself with indolent grace in the chair indicated and crossing one leg over his knee as he stretched his arms casually along the back of the seat. Looking at him like this she couldn't believe that he had been married, that he had a home, a daughter, any sort of domesticated life. He was the epitome of the eternal bachelor, the lone wolf with no ties or commitments. But she had *seen* him with Alexandra. Seen the unaffected devotion that marked his handling of his tiny daughter, the gentleness, the love... She felt that familiar stark churning in her stomach and turned away sharply, her head whirling. He was several different men in one skin, that was the only way she could reconcile the differences in his diverse personality, and with her there would be a totally different set of ground rules to those governing his relationship with Alexandra. He found her physically attractive, in a purely carnal sense, and would be content to indulge his bodily lust until such time as he either tired of her or moved on out of her tiny sphere,. She knew that. *She knew it.* So why did she allow this sensual domination of her senses? She was an intelligent sensible person in her own right; it was totally illogical to let him intimidate her like this.

'Would you like a drink?' She indicated the minibar in the corner of the room. 'I was just going to have a mineral water.'

'Sounds good.' Just for a moment, a fleeting moment, she got the impression he was finding this whole situation as difficult as she was, but she dismissed it instantly as she gave him his drink. Logan Steer unsure of himself? Whatever had put such a thought in her mind? She really was going mad!

'Marmalade is gradually getting the others into shape.' Logan smiled drily as she seated herself gingerly on the very edge of the chair opposite, her robe tucked carefully into place and her knees tightly together. 'My housekeeper informs me that Dee and Tabitha were instant pushovers but the dogs took a bit longer.'

'Is he behaving?' she asked anxiously.

'Impeccably, from what I can gather.' The dark face was very cool and she could read nothing from his expression to indicate what he was feeling. Was he aware of this emotion that was pulsing in the very air between them, an energy, a force, that was purely sensual and frighteningly erotic? She could feel her face was flushed and warm but there was nothing she could do about that; it was taking all her willpower to hide the trembling that was shuddering in her stomach. It shocked her that she could feel like this, that she wondered, whenever she was with him, what it would be like to be loved by such a man and, worse, how it would be if her soft female body fused with the hardness of his...

'You should have stayed for coffee.' His deep rich voice brought her eyes snapping to meet the silver-blue gaze. 'Giles would have liked it.'

'I was tired.' She shrugged carefully and indicated the robe with a quick wave of her hand. 'I was just going to have a shower and go to bed when you arrived.'

'Please don't let me stop you,' he said seriously without a flicker of a smile. 'I'm pretty adept at scrubbing backs, if you feel like any help? And Dee swears by my tucking-in technique.'

'I'm sure she does.' She eyed him grimly. 'But I don't happen to be a four-year-old child and you don't happen to be my father, Logan.'

'True.' Now there was a definite gleam of wickedness in the silver gaze. 'Unadventurous, unsporting even, but true. Are you going to let me show you some of the sights while we're here?'

The abrupt change in conversation threw her for a moment and she stared at him blankly as the phone next to her chair rang in a low discreet burble. She picked it up automatically and then, as Paul's familiar voice spoke into her ear, felt a rush of overwhelming relief.

'Melly? How are things? Settled in yet? I thought I'd give you a ring before it got too late.' The cheerful voice brought an immediate mental picture of Paul's square good-looking face with its neatly cut fair hair and serious pale blue eyes that always made her feel there was nordic blood somewhere in his background. 'I'm just finishing some work on my correspondence course.'

'Paul...' As her eyes rose and met Logan's glittering ice-blue gaze across the room, the contrast between the two men hit her as forcibly as if Paul were in the room with them and suddenly her voice died at the expression on Logan's face.

'Melly?' Paul's voice held a note of anxiety now. 'Is everything all right?'

'Yes, yes, everything's fine,' she said quickly as she wrenched her eyes away from the dark sardonic face opposite her. 'I'm just a bit tired tonight, that's all. Giles has insisted on a full day's work in spite of the travelling.'

'Well, he's got deadlines to meet,' Paul said practically. It was true, Giles had, but the lack of sympathy suddenly hit a little nerve and she couldn't imagine why. 'This wasn't meant to be a holiday, after all.'

'No.' Logan was making no effort to leave, in fact he seemed to have settled further into the chair, but the hard tanned face was quite expressionless as she searched desperately for something to say. 'How are things in England?' she asked weakly.

'The same as when you left this morning.' Typical Paul, she thought wryly, logical to the last.

'Missing me?' She didn't know why she spoke the words, or used the light teasing tone. Perhaps it was something to do with the almost smug blandness of Logan's face as he listened to her end of the conversation. Whatever, Paul's voice held a note of almost comical surprise when he next spoke.

'Well, I've been working on my correspondence course all evening.' He paused and, although the phone was silent, she smiled suggestively into the receiver as though the words she was hearing from the other end were wonderfully to her liking. 'And I've got to go and visit Mother this weekend—you know she likes me there on the first weekend in the month.'

'Ummm...' She let her voice trail away in a manner that could have been an answer to anything and was inordinately pleased when Logan's gaze became steel-like. Tepid friendship? she thought grimly. Well, maybe, Mr Steer, but you can just wonder a little, can't you! Why should you think you've got the monopoly on sex and

romance anyway? And surely, if he thought his
judgement of her relationship with Paul had been wrong,
he would back off? Do the right thing? Leave the field
clear for the younger man? He could have any woman
he wanted after all; it was only some perverse sexual
pride that was making him bother with her in the first
place. Like a collector of precious stones, with hundreds
at his disposal, going after the one unobtainable piece
for the thrill of conquest.

'Have you...?' Paul's voice faltered in uncustomary
diffidence. 'Have you seen much of this chap Steer, by
the way?'

'A little.' A little too much, she thought balefully.
What Paul's reaction would be if he could see her sitting
stark naked under a light towelling robe drinking with
Logan in her hotel room she wouldn't like to imagine!
But perhaps his response would be as lukewarm as most
of his emotions seemed to be? She froze as the thought
took form in her mind, horrified at the betrayal. But it
was true. She almost shut her eyes to blot out the still
small voice in her mind that was relentlessly persistent.
Paul was a company man, devoted to his work and office
credibility, with everything else in his life coming a very
definite second. The only time she had ever known him
to get excited was when he had received a personal com-
mendation from Giles on a particular project he had been
in charge of. Indeed, Giles seemed to treat him as a pet
puppy half of the time. And Logan? She glanced again
at the long lean body and granite-hard face. No. Not
even Giles would be foolish enough to presume to tell
Logan what to do. By why was she thinking like this?
Her mind snapped back to Paul who had launched into
an involved monologue on a problem in his correspondence course that he had tackled and overcome. She'd

go mad if she had to listen to another word with Logan watching her face with those piercingly intuitive eyes of his.

'Well, bye for now.' She spoke quickly as Paul paused for breath. 'This must be costing you a fortune. You really musn't phone every day, Paul.' It was purely for Logan's benefit again. Knowing Paul as she did, she knew he wouldn't dream of wasting money in such an unnecessary fashion. 'But it was very sweet of you to be concerned.'

'I wasn't concerned,' Paul said in surprise. 'I just wanted to know how things were going. Giles has mentioned that he might want me over in the last stages to tie up the purchasing details.'

'That'd be lovely.' She forced a low laugh and watched Logan's eyes turn glacial. 'Take care, then.'

'Yes.' For the first time in their relationship she could tell that Paul was slightly out of his depth and she couldn't really blame him. He must be wondering if she'd been over-indulging in French wine, she thought almost hysterically. 'Well, I'll talk to you again in a few days. Goodnight, Melly.' Not exactly the farewell of an ardent suitor, she thought drily as she made an appropriate response and put down the telephone, but then no one in his right mind could ever pin that description on Paul's narrow shoulders.

'That was——'

'Paul. Yes, I know.' Logan cut into her breathless voice smoothly, his face cool and aloof. 'He's quite a dedicated fan of Giles, isn't he?'

'What does that mean?' Melly asked warily.

'Exactly what I said.' The deep voice was drawling and lazy but there was an undertone of cutting mockery that grated on her overwrought nerves like wire wool.

'He really won't do, Melly, not at all. Having fitted a face and body to the name, I'm even more sure Paul isn't for you.'

'Oh, are you indeed?' She felt pure undiluted rage replace the blood in her veins. 'Well, to earn your disapproval he's got to have a lot going for him, that's for sure. Your opinion is the very last one I'd ever take any notice of.'

'What a little firebrand you are.' His customary lazy amusement seemed to have deserted him for once. Although his voice was still relaxed and drawling there was a definite edge that had been absent before and the stony eyes were harsh and cold.

He had to be the most egotistical man she had ever met, Melly thought angrily as she stared back unwaveringly into the handsome cruel face. Just because she had resisted him in the final analysis all those years ago, he had to prove to himself that he could have her if he wanted and, worse, that no other man was as worthy as him. Egomaniac was positively anaemic when applied to him! 'Firebrand?' She faced him furiously. 'Because I object to you poking your nose in where it isn't wanted? Other women might go weak at the knees before your charm, Logan, but not me! Definitely not me. I know exactly where you're coming from and you don't fool me for a minute. You can keep all the advice and the concern because I'm not interested. I know what you're really like.'

'Do you indeed?' He had risen when she did and now they stood just inches apart like two gladiators preparing to enter the ring. 'And what, exactly, have you based this knowledge on?'

'You don't need me to spell it out.' She glared at him angrily. 'You're not so old that senility has set in——'

'Right, that's it!' His face had grown blacker and blacker over the last few minutes but she had been too incensed to care, but now, as he pulled her into his arms with a frenzied strength that spoke eloquently of his boiling temper, she found herself wishing she had taken heed of the warning. She was alone with him in her hotel room, virtually naked, and she knew from the past that this man was a completely unprincipled opportunist where women were concerned. She should have kept cool and aloof and sent him packing at the earliest opportunity, not enter a war of words that she could never win. And now he was angry, furiously angry, and that cold hard control that was ever present in everything he said and did had totally blown.

He seemed to devour her mouth, waves of temper spreading the fire that had him in its hold dangerously, and she was completely helpless in his grasp, realising for the first time the power in his hard big body. She couldn't move, all her struggles quietened as effectively as though she were in a steel vice, and as his mouth, urgent and hungry, continued to wreak havoc on her face and throat she was horrified to find a hot burning pleasure beginning to seep into the pit of her stomach. She couldn't respond to him, not now, like this, when everything he was doing was meant as a punishment for her defiance! But although her brain was resisting, her body had taken the traitor's course, working with him to drag her down into a well of potent hot desire. And she sensed he knew it.

She wasn't aware that the robe had fallen open but suddenly, as he shuddered in a violent paroxysm of passion, he moved her from him with an almost desperate gesture of repudiation and she realised, in that stunning second before her senses returned in full flood, that she was wearing little more than her dignity.

As she pulled the edges of the robe together, knotting the belt with shaking numb hands, she raised her burning face to him and almost spat the words into his dark face. 'Don't you ever do that again, Logan, I mean it. I might have to work with you but that doesn't mean I like it and, whatever you may think from the past, I'm not easy game. Do you hear me?' She had almost screamed the last words, her control shot to a thousand pieces, and as he looked at her the expression on his face silenced any further insults she had been about to throw as effectively as a gag. He looked as devastated as she felt and suddenly, against all rhyme or reason, she felt all the fury drain out of her in a painful rush and searing hot anguish take its place as the look changed to something approaching pain.

He made as though to speak, but then he strode across the room without a word, opening the door and disappearing into the corridor outside before she could draw breath, the door banging shut behind him with a flat, empty sound. He had gone.

As her legs buckled she sank straight down on to the soft inch-thick carpet in a trembling, shaking rush, unable to comprehend the anger and emotion of the last few minutes. Why did he continue to affect her like this? In such an elemental, searingly earthy way? Everything about him touched a sharp nerve in her body; even when they were in company and he was urbane, quiet and controlled the trigger was there, in every movement, every flick of those cool hooded eyes. And that last glance he had given her... There had been a dark angry pain in its depths that had gripped her heart like an iron hand and squeezed the breath out of her body.

As she wrapped her arms round her legs and swayed back and forth on the floor like a small distressed animal she fought the hot tears pricking at the backs of her eyes with all her might. She would *not* cry over this man again. There had been too much of that in the far distant past and it would do no good. She had to fight strength with strength, anger with anger. She couldn't afford the luxury of tears, she *wouldn't* allow them. He might think he had the whip-hand but she would show him that brute force was no victory. And her body's betrayal to his? She bit her lip hard until the taste of blood was in her mouth. That was another warning and she would take full heed of it. She had been foolish tonight, foolish and weak to allow him entry into her room, but she would make sure in the future that they were never alone together for a second.

As Melly walked down to breakfast the following morning careful use of cosmetics had hidden most of the evidence of a sleepless night and, on the surface at least, she appeared businesslike and composed. She was early, she had planned to be. She fully intended to be sitting enjoying breakfast without a care in the world when Logan made his appearance in the hotel dining-room.

He arrived just a minute or two after her and joined her at the otherwise empty table with a tight nod. 'I knocked on your door a moment ago but when there was no answer I assumed you were here.'

'Did you?' She raised veiled eyes to meet his gaze. She had seen him as he had walked in and dropped her eyes immediately, but not before a hard physical jolt had ricocheted through her chest with dreadful suddenness.

'I wanted to apologise for last night's fiasco,' he continued grimly. 'I have never lost my temper with a woman before and my behaviour was inexcusable.'

'Oh...' The unexpectedness and obvious genuineness of the apology left her floundering for words. She had spent most of the night doing endless post-mortems on every word spoken and unspoken between them since he had entered the room and in the cold early hours had been forced to admit that the blame was not solely on his shoulders. In setting up Paul as a defence against his supposed seduction she had probably made a difficult situation ten times worse, but that didn't excuse either his aggressive hostility where Paul was concerned or his bitingly cold mockery.

'Are you prepared to accept my apology, Melly, or would you like me to put things right with Giles and allow you to leave without any danger to your job?' he asked, still in the same tight strained voice.

She looked at him levelly over the vase of fresh flowers on the white linen tablecloth. 'And what exactly would you say, Logan?' she asked flatly. 'Nothing that could be helpful to either of our careers and certainly not to my reputation. I don't think Giles is the type of man to appreciate personal difficulties getting in the way of a project of his, do you?'

'Possibly not.' He gestured irritably as he ran a hand through his wiry black hair. 'But I'd deal with Giles in my own way.'

'I accept your apology.' She crumbled the end of a croissant between her fingers as she spoke, her eyes downwards. 'I'm here to do a job and I've never yet walked out on anything I've committed myself to. I'd prefer to forget last night.' Her heart was thudding a loud tattoo but, amazingly, the trembling that was affecting her body was not reflected in her voice and there was dead silence at the table for a long heart-stoppingly tense moment.

'Thank you.' His voice was icy, polite and distant. 'I give you my word I won't force myself on you again.'

The arrival of the others through the doorway of the dining-room effectively finished further conversation and, as Melly forced herself slowly to eat the croissant, followed by a hot cup of coffee, the shivery sensation in her stomach gradually diminished. She looked everywhere but at Logan. There was no way she could handle meeting those cool blue eyes without betraying her inner agitation and it was vitally important to her pride and her self-respect that she appeared relaxed and self-controlled.

That morning set the pace for the next two weeks. They established an acceptable working relationship that was by necessity of what had gone before cold and formal, and when Logan mentioned Marmalade, as he did after his phone calls to England, it was only in the barest of terms and always with at least one other person present.

And she hated it. Alone in her room at night she would berate herself over and over again for her inconsistency but there was no getting away from the fact: this indifferent, reserved and imperturbable attitude of Logan's was hurting, and hurting badly. It was ridiculous—more than ridiculous, criminally stupid—but somehow she felt as though she was mourning the loss of something vitally precious she had never had in the first place. She couldn't understand herself and that was driving her mad. Paul's voice on the other end of the phone in his infrequent phone calls had the effect of making her want to scream and the constant never-ending grind of hard work was making her exhausted and irritable.

And that was the state of affairs on the Friday afternoon when they had been in Paris just over two weeks. She was in the middle of typing a sensitive financial report with Giles peering over her shoulder, a practice she hated, when Logan strolled indolently into the room through Giles's room after a cursory knock. She had hardly set foot out of the hotel in the two weeks she had been in Paris and, as Logan glanced at her, he noticed both her pallor and the tight line of her mouth.

'I'm stealing Melly for the weekend, OK, Giles?' he asked lazily as both Melly's head and her boss's snapped up to meet his. 'She needs a break and I've promised to visit Alexandra this weekend—she'll think it strange if I don't bring Melly to see the cat.'

'The cat?' Giles asked vaguely before nodding his head sharply. 'Oh, yes, the cat. Sure, sure, the break'll do her good. I've been working her pretty hard but the worst is over now.'

If they carried on discussing her like this with a blind disregard for the fact that she was present, living and breathing, she would do something that they would *all* regret, Melly thought angrily as she glanced up at the men's faces.

'OK, Melly?' Right on cue Logan glanced straight at her and the blue eyes were as clear and as sharp as glass. He knew exactly what she was going to say, Melly thought silently, she could read it in the very blandness of the hard features looking back at her. 'Dee did say in her last call that Marmalade was a little restless. Probably needs a spot of reassurance that you are still on the planet.' He smiled without it touching his eyes.

'I don't think so——' she began quickly, but he cut in on her, his voice patient and surprised and holding just the right amount of careful disapproval.

'Surely you can spare a few hours to reassure a cat and please a child?' he asked condemningly. 'It'll only be a twenty-four-hour trip and I'm sure there's nothing that won't wait here?' He raised enquiring eyes to Giles who shook his head quickly.

'Absolutely, old man, do you both the world of good. I might do something similar actually, have a night on the town if I can drag old Alfred out.' He smiled at them both genially.

Melly looked at them and admitted defeat. If ever she had needed a break in her life she needed one now. For some reason she was all at sixes and sevens with herself and everyone else and a brief visit to see Marmalade would do her no harm...would it? She glanced at Logan's bland face and felt slightly reassured. He had made it clear over the last two weeks that he could turn off this strange physical attraction he had felt for her with no trouble. She felt a little dart of something sharp in her heart region. And that was what she wanted, of course she did. So there was no problem?

'All right, thank you.' Melly felt a moment's unease at a sudden flash of something hot in Logan's eyes but then, as she looked again, they were their usual cool untroubled blue, hard and unfathomable, and she decided she must have imagined it. But that was how he affected her, she thought crossly. She was never sure of anything round him.

'The tickets are booked for the nine o'clock flight to-morrow evening,' Logan said over his shoulder as he strolled out of the room, 'and I thought we'd go out to dinner tonight, Melly, at a little place I know. I'll give you a knock about seven so there's no rush.'

He had gone before she could react and, as she glanced dumbly at Giles, her eyes narrowed and frowning, the older man shrugged his broad shoulders matter-of-factly. 'He'd already booked the tickets?' she said abruptly. 'What if I'd refused to go?'

'Logan doesn't take no for an answer if he wants something.' Giles's tone was almost expressionless and as she looked up at him she felt he was trying to tell her something more than the mere words suggested.

'Doesn't he?' she said grimly. 'Well, one day he might have a rude awakening at such high-handed methods.'

'Maybe.' Giles's tone indicated his sympathies were all with Logan and she gave up further conversation, concentrating on the report and finishing it quickly and efficiently.

Dinner. She grimaced at herself later as she stood under the warm shower in her room. Give him an inch and he took a mile! What did he want to have dinner with her for anyway? She ignored the pounding of her heart and excited fluttering in her stomach with iron determination. Well, she'd made it perfectly clear where they stood and his attitude over the last few days had shown her that his attraction to her had been casual and easily put aside. If he wanted them to get on a more acceptably friendly footing it could only help their work, and no doubt that was exactly his own thought.

Nevertheless, she paid more than a little attention to her toilette, creaming expensive body lotion into every inch of smooth unlined flesh and applying a light touch of eyeshadow and mascara to darken and widen her large eyes.

It was the first week of October now and the evenings were still pleasantly warm, but the light long full-skirted dress she chose to wear in a pale blue cotton had a matching jacket that she slung over her arm as she heard his knock at the door.

She took a deep breath before she opened the door, her stomach whirling. This didn't mean a thing, not a thing, she told herself firmly as she reached for the handle. It was a social gesture, a desire to banish the tension that had existed over the last two weeks, that was all.

'Melly.' Like that other time he detached himself lazily from the opposite wall and moved slowly towards her, and instantly her senses went into hyper-drive. Devastatingly casual in an open-necked black silk shirt teamed with loose grey cotton trousers he looked every inch the dark debonair Frenchman out for a night in sultry Paris, and every instinct in her screamed caution. 'You look absolutely gorgeous.' One hand had been behind his back and now he handed her a tiny box with a little bow. 'I saw this a couple of days ago and couldn't resist. You'll see why.'

She looked at him weakly and then opened the lid of the box cautiously. A present? 'Oh, Logan...' She raised smiling eyes to his. She had been afraid of an expensive ostentatious gift, an offering with a thousand strings attached, but the perfect little ginger cat was obviously inexpensive and an exact replica of Marmalade down to the huge green eyes that stared at her with a definitely superior expression in their depths. 'It's him.' He fastened the enamel brooch expertly on to her dress.

'Quite.' Logan smiled at her approval. 'It looked at me so disdainfully it couldn't have been anyone else.'

'It's lovely, thank you.' As she smiled up at him she had the strangest feeling that the two of them were surrounded by a silver aura, a sparkle of light, but in the next instant as she blinked the impression died.

'Shall we go?' he asked smoothly, his eyes cool and his face remote. Nevertheless, as she smiled and took the arm he offered, the previous misgivings returned a hundredfold and, as they left the hotel and strolled out into the warm scented night, he took her hand in his in a casual relaxed manner that was entirely natural but caused her stomach to do an immediate somersault. This was Logan, *Logan*. The only man to have seen her naked, *twice*, the man who had nearly wrecked her life once and would do so again without a moment's hesitation if it suited his purpose, an opportunist, a dangerous adversary, a...

'Friends again?' As he smiled down into her eyes she nodded dazedly and almost missed her footing, causing his hand to tighten on hers.

She was crazy, mad, foolish, but... She took a deep breath of the shadowed perfumed air and felt wonderfully alive. This was just one night. She would have just one night...

# CHAPTER SIX

THEY walked slowly along the winding street, hand in hand, like a thousand other young couples in this magical city of love. The sky was black velvet, pierced with stars and flooded with an ethereal allure that turned the soft evening air into misty shadows. Melly had ceased to think; she was taking this night minute by minute, a lone solitary step out of her life that wouldn't be repeated and therefore was allowed to be enjoyed to the full. Because it would be too dangerous to do this again. She glanced up at Logan's dark handsome profile and again her heart gave that queer little kick. Much too dangerous.

There were innumerable bars and cafés spilling out on to the old pavements and almost every other building was a restaurant where whole families of Parisians sat enjoying the night air under gaily striped umbrellas outside or with the doors to the restaurant wide open. The smells that floated on the moist warm air were deliciously tempting and more than once Melly found her mouth watering as they passed by.

On either side of the Seine illuminated buildings added a fairy-tale enchantment to the capital's busy nightlife, the sound of music drifting from brightly lit restaurants as they strolled by. A lazy, languid kind of pleasure seemed to have taken hold of Melly's senses and she didn't try to fight it. For once she was going with the flow and it was intoxicating.

'I found this restaurant the very first time I came to Paris years ago,' Logan said quietly after a time. 'It's just round the next corner. It didn't seem worth taking a cab, besides which——' he paused and drew her into his side '—the walk is rather nice, don't you think?'

She nodded without speaking—the warm unguarded expression in those normally piercingly cool eyes had taken away her power of speech.

And the restaurant was delightful. From the outside it looked exactly the same as hundreds of others in similar streets that wound all over the Latin Quarter, but once in the dimly lit interior she saw that the building was built round a central courtyard that was open to the stars with a fountain splashing down on to a massive illuminated pool full of exotically coloured fish, with wonderfully perfumed vegetation scenting the air with a thousand summer perfumes. The owner had made the most of the unusual design and the inner wall surrounding the courtyard consisted of large glass doors that slid away to let the courtyard blend with the restaurant when the weather permitted. The whole effect was one of timeless enchantment and picturesque beauty and, as she sipped a cocktail while Logan consulted with the waitress, she found herself wondering how many women he had brought here. Probably hundreds! The exaggeration didn't cause a moment of guilt.

'You're frowning.' She hadn't realised he had finished talking with the plump young girl but now her eyes left the courtyard abruptly and fastened on his dark tanned face, to find his eyes quizzical. 'What have I done wrong now?'

'It doesn't have to be something you've done wrong, does it?' she prevaricated quickly as her skin burnt hotly.

'No?' He settled back in his seat and surveyed her through narrowed eyes. 'Come on then, tell me what you were thinking and prove a point.'

She shrugged gracefully and then decided to play him at his own game. He wanted honesty? So be it. 'I was wondering how many other women you've brought here, actually,' she said sweetly. 'That's all.'

He straightened abruptly in his seat and she was gratified to see that for once she had totally surprised him. 'Were you?' He stared at her intently for a long minute and then smiled carefully. 'And how many did you decide?'

'Oh, hundreds,' she said airily.

'I see.' She knew he didn't like it but he obviously decided to treat the matter lightly, his mouth smiling even as his eyes remained a cool silver-blue. 'You flatter me.'

'Do I?' She smiled with mocking surprise. 'I do apologise, I didn't intend to!' And as her eyebrows rose in sharp irony, her mouth wry, she saw him stiffen and then visibly relax a moment later as he gave a low mordant chuckle.

'You little vixen.' He eyed her warily but the smile was genuine now and suddenly, at his easy acceptance of the joke against himself, she felt something move and melt in her that frightened her to death. What was she doing? *What was she doing*? Flirting with him? Pretending he was a man like any other? But he wasn't. She knew he wasn't.

The waitress's arrival with the first course broke the moment but her heart was thudding for several minutes afterwards. Come on, Melly, you're a big girl now, she told herself silently as she began on the *crudités variées* Logan had ordered, a mixture of deliciously crisp raw vegetables in oil and vinegar. We're already nearly halfway through the six weeks allotted for Paris and then you needn't ever see Logan again. Funnily enough, the thought didn't give her the boost she needed. In fact just the opposite.

The food was absolutely delicious and as course followed course with a different glass of wine to complement each one Melly found herself gradually relaxing. She was too serious, she decided firmly after the third glass of wine. Too intense; it had to stop. 'This is delicious.' She gestured at the chicken with tarragon that was melting in her mouth. 'What's in it?'

Logan's eyes wandered slowly over her flushed cheeks before he replied, his gaze warm and heavy on her half-open lips. 'Obviously chicken and tarragon,' he said quietly, 'along with butter, spices, egg yolk, fresh cream...all kinds of goodies.'

'And what's next?' She smiled appreciatively. 'I like your taste in food, Logan.'

'Well, that's something.' The sardonic voice was gently mocking. 'But I thought food was the way to a man's heart, not a woman's?'

'Wrong, definitely wrong.' She giggled suddenly and then realised with a little start of surprise that she was slightly tipsy. This glass of wine was definitely the last, she decided, as she took a tiny sip that barely lowered the level in the glass. She needed *all* her faculties around Logan.

By the time she had eaten the last scrap of a *mystère*, a wickedly creamy vanilla ice-cream with meringue in the middle and chopped nuts on the outside, she was wonderfully replete.

'That was gorgeous, Logan, thank you very much,' she said quietly as they sat sipping coffee and watching the fountain cascade in a hundred shattered colours into the moving pool beneath, the low hum of conversation from the tables scattered around the central courtyard tantalisingly foreign.

'Very polite.' She looked up quickly but the dark face wasn't mocking, merely gently teasing and almost...almost tender? She kicked herself mentally. Don't start imagining things, Melly, she told herself grimly. 'Did your mother always instruct you to say please and thank you?' he asked softly.

'Of course.' She looked at him guardedly. 'Didn't yours?'

He hesitated for a long moment and then spoke very matter-of-factly, his eyes veiled and opaque in the dim light. 'I was brought up in a succession of foster homes from the age of three,' he said quietly, 'and the rules seemed to be different in each one. I sorted out my own set of dos and don'ts quite early but unfortunately they sometimes didn't sit too well in individual households.' He smiled slowly.

'What happened to your parents?' she asked dazedly, stunned by the unexpected confidence. Logan? In a string of different homes from a toddler? She couldn't have believed how much the picture in her mind hurt.

'My father took off long before I was born,' he said expressionlessly. 'He hadn't married my mother. She stayed around until I was three but then decided she wanted her freedom.' He shrugged slowly. 'It happens all the time, it's no big deal. She kept in touch now and again but she died a few years ago, just before Alexandra was born.'

'So she never saw her grandchild?' Melly said quietly.

'I don't think she would have displayed much interest anyway,' Logan said drily after a pregnant pause. 'She wasn't exactly the maternal type. She liked me much better when I was an adult.'

'Did you love her?' It was a personal question but the wine had loosened her tongue. He paused again, and then looked straight at her, his face cold.

'I didn't even like her,' he said coolly, 'or the little I knew about her anyway. I was a biological result of her brief union with my father, that much was fact, but as far as any rapport went...' He stopped abruptly. 'Well, there was none. From the age of three to sixteen I saw her a handful of times, if that, but when she discovered I was tall for my age and reasonably presentable it amused her to introduce me to her friends as her son. I didn't click on at first——' again that brief pause '— but when I finally realised I was being used I decided enough was enough, as they say.' He eyed her expressionlessly.

'But perhaps it wasn't as you thought?' She looked hard into the closed dark face. 'You might have misjudged her, Logan.'

'No.' He smiled slowly at her flushed earnest face but the bitterness in his eyes caused her stomach to twist. 'I didn't misjudge her.'

'But how do you *know*?' she persisted quietly. 'Her behaviour through the years had obviously hurt you; perhaps you were the last person in the world to judge——'

'I know because she arranged for one of her friends, who had a penchant for young boys, to seduce me,' he said in a dull distant tone as he turned from her and stared out across the glittering fountain. 'Fortunately the man in her life at the time hadn't the stomach for it and he told me what was going on. When I confronted her she was most put out that I should object. I'm sorry, Melly, but she wasn't a nice woman.' His eyes returned to her shocked face. 'An accident of birth made her my mother but she was totally devoid of any maternal feeling. You can get women like that.'

'I'm sorry, Logan.' She didn't know what to say. She would never have dreamed that anything that had happened so long ago, and not even to her, could hurt quite so much, or that she could feel such murderous rage against a woman she had never even met and was now dead.

'It's all right.' He bent forward suddenly and took the hand that was gripping her coffee-cup with rigid tautness, smoothing out her stiff fingers in his open palm as he looked into her troubled brown eyes. 'I should never have told you, Melly. I'm sorry, it wasn't fair to burden you with that and it was a long time ago. I don't know why I *did* tell you. I've never discussed it with anyone else.' The deep hard voice held a note of faint surprise in its depths.

'How could someone be like that?' she asked weakly as the feel of his warm flesh sent goose-pimples all over her body.

'It was part and parcel of the world in which she lived,' he said quietly. 'The whole of her set were always seeking new diversions, new excitement. They were hooked on practically everything it's possible to be addicted to: drugs, drink, sex, and the more unusual the better was the key. And yet from the outside they appeared just to be having a good time. The rot from within was difficult to see. The idea had been that I was to be handed around, like a new toy, and in spite of being a tough kid, and street-wise, I would have been taken in. It was my mother after all. As it was, the whole incident gave me the impetus I needed to apply my brains and aim for university, so I suppose you could say in a strange sort of way she did me a favour even if it was a kick in the teeth at the time.'

'But if you'd gone through that, if they'd made you feel...' She stopped abruptly. 'Why did you try...?' She stopped again.

'How could I have tried to seduce you?' he asked softly, reading her mind with uncanny perception. 'I didn't, Melly, believe me, not in the way you thought then and still do. When I got to university I suppose I went slightly mad for a time. There were all these girls...crazy young girls. Girls who were obviously attracted to me and weren't afraid to show it. So I admit I was foolish for a time, but only a time and not as much as you seem to think. I had a few girlfriends, we all did, but the grapevine made more of it and I have to admit I didn't altogether object to the image of Jack the Lad. It seemed to reduce some of the humiliation I'd carried since the incident when I was sixteen. But I finished with Lauren, if you remember, when I found out she was playing fast and loose. That sort of game is not my style, Melly; it never has been.' She wanted to believe him. Suddenly she wanted to so much. 'And I had no intention of seducing you that night. But you were so damn sweet...' He looked at her in the dim light. 'And lovely and innocent... Everything I'd ever wanted.'

'Logan...' She moved her hand from his abruptly. This was happening too fast, and he couldn't know what he was doing to her. This attraction between them, it was just a physical thing, *that was all*, but it was so powerful that she couldn't afford to weaken where he was concerned. It didn't matter about the past in a way, the present was more than she could deal with. Did she trust him? She looked into the devastatingly male face that was hard and dark and vitally handsome. She didn't know, she wasn't sure.

He drew back immediately at the panic in her face, his eyes suddenly veiled. 'Time to go.' He smiled carefully. 'I'm taking you to Montmartre tomorrow before we leave for England, so you'll need your beauty sleep tonight.'

'Montmartre?' She felt dizzy at the speed in which the last few hours had seemed to change everything after two weeks of hard work and unchanging routine.

'On the first Saturday in October they have the grape harvest,' he said quietly, 'a wine festival celebrating the last remaining wine produced in Paris. There are wine auctions, parades through Montmartre ... It's fun.' He smiled sardonically but it reassured her somewhat to see the old cynical Logan back in place. 'You do know about fun?' he asked drily. 'I can imagine it's not a word that comes easily to Paul.'

She made an appropriately scathing reply but her heart wasn't really in it, and on the walk back to the hotel through the noisy colourful streets full of nightlife there seemed to be courting couples everywhere, on every street corner, in every shadowed arch. There was none of the easy informality of their earlier stroll. This time Logan was careful not to touch her and she felt acutely put out even as she chastised herself for her fickleness.

Once in the hotel outside her room she looked up at him as she felt in her handbag for her key. 'Thank you for tonight, Logan——'

'You've already said that once.' His voice was thick as he interrupted her and as he took her in his arms, smoothing a wispy curl from her forehead as he bent to take her lips, she could feel herself melting into his hard body in immediate submission. The kiss was restrained and cool as though he was exerting an iron control on his emotions, but even so she felt herself begin to tremble at the sensations it produced. It only lasted a matter of seconds but by the time he moved her gently from him her heart was thumping and her legs were weak. Stupid, stupid, stupid, she told herself with furious self-disgust, but it made no difference. He only had to touch her and he seemed to trigger a whirlwind of sensation over which she had no control at all. And it horrified her that she could feel like that about a man she barely knew, didn't trust and wasn't even sure if she liked. Why, up until a few weeks ago she had loathed the very thought of his name! So why did this physical attraction continue despite all the cold logic she could bring to bear against it? And why had the revelations about his younger years hurt so much? It didn't make sense. Nothing did any more.

'Your key?' She realised he had moved back a pace and was standing looking down at her with an unreadable expression colouring the remote blue eyes silver.

As her fingers found the key in her handbag she handed it to him without a word as a cold little shiver slipped down her spine. He was coming into her room. This, then, was the big seduction scene? The finale of all the soft words, tender glances and brief glimpse into his past he had allowed her this night? She should have known. She *should* have known. And what was she going to do about it?

She never had the chance to find out. As she handed him the key he unlocked her door in one easy movement, deposited a brief kiss of farewell on the top of her head, pushed her gently into the room as he placed the key back in her nerveless fingers and switched on the light and then he was gone, the door closing firmly behind him as he turned and left.

'I don't believe this.' As she stared at the closed door she had the sudden urge to burst out into hysterical laughter. He must have known how she felt. She had been unable to hide her reaction to the kiss, so why...? She frowned at the blank wood vacantly. She didn't attract him any more. Or not enough to risk another rebuff anyway, and she couldn't blame him. She remembered the last time he had been in her room and winced visibly. She had made it crystal-clear how she felt about him and he had taken note. He had wanted a brief physical fling and she hadn't been prepared to play ball. End of story as far as he was concerned. She bit her lip hard. And that was perfect, *perfect*, exactly how she wanted it. She nodded sharply. And she had been right earlier: the tension of the last two weeks was not conducive to good working relations and he had been trying to put things on a more even footing. Hence the meal tonight and little trip tomorrow to Montmartre before they left for England. Good. She stared forlornly round the empty room and bit back savagely on the sudden urge to burst into tears. Everything was so... perfect.

Pavement artists were at work in picturesque Montmartre when they arrived by taxi the next morning, and, after arranging for the cheerful taxi-driver to return in time to pick up their overnight cases before driving them to the airport, Logan took Melly's arm and drew her into the noisy throng lining a sun-filled square as they watched a group of actors portraying the harvest in mime and song.

It was a wonderful day. The narrow streets and cobbles of hilly Montmartre surrounded the Sacré Coeur like

the decoration on a giant wedding cake from which the
beautiful building, with its domed roofs, arched windows
and exquisite stonework, rose like the majestic centre-
piece. And everywhere the emphasis was on wine. From
the wine auctions, gay affairs with an undertone of
deadly bargaining, the colourful parades through the
ancient streets and the carnival-like atmosphere that
prevailed, to the numerous little cafés and restaurants
decked out festively as though in a last fling before the
onset of winter. Even the weather had joined in the
carefree gala spirit, Melly reflected silently, as she sat
sipping a glass of rich fruity red wine outside a little café
with Logan, watching the world go by as they waited
for their teatime snack of fresh toasted sandwiches. The
October day was warm and sunny and heady with the
scent of autumn flowers that seemed to cascade from
every window-box and tiny garden.

'Enjoying it?' As Logan bent forward and raised her
hand to his lips for a fleeting moment before turning
back in lazy surveillance of the scene before him, her
heart bounded crazily out of beat for a second before
righting itself again. Was he as aware of her as she was
of him? she thought painfully as she watched the big
dark loose-limbed body out of the corner of her eye.
The black jeans and casual shirt he was wearing made
him younger today somehow, as well as emphasising the
broadness of the powerful shoulders and strong chest.
He exuded sensuality, she thought weakly, it just flowed
from him in an earthy, vigorous, totally virile mass that
made her stomach muscles tight and the palms of her
hands damp. And she wasn't the only female to be affected either. It shouldn't bother her that almost every
female head that passed swung sharply for another look
but it did. Dammit, *it did*, she acknowledged tensely,

shutting her eyes for a moment as she fought with the
irritation her weakness produced.

'You're very beautiful.' As his voice, low and deep,
brought her eyes snapping open she saw he had turned
in his seat to face her, his back to the moving scene
beyond. 'Very beautiful and very nervous.'

'Nervous?' She reared up instantly, her chestnut hair
a burnished mass of curls in the white sunlight. 'I'm not
nervous.'

'No?' He stretched out his long legs as he idly took
a sip of wine, his eyes narrowed and thoughtful as they
rested on her flushed face. 'I'm sorry, Melly, but I don't
believe you. For some reason you're like a cat on a hot
tin roof round me. I'd like to think it was flattering but
the thought intrudes that it's a case of give a dog a bad
name and hang him. You don't trust me an inch, do
you? You expect any moment that I'm going to launch
some kind of attack——'

'Don't be ridiculous.' She eyed him as coolly as she
could considering her cheeks were burning scarlet. 'I'm
not into playing love games, that's all. The sophisticated
kiss-and-run technique has never appealed to me.'

'Nor me.' The dark face was deadly serious. 'Is that
what you think? That I'm the type of man who will have
the odd affair and move on to the next woman without
a qualm?' She stared at him without speaking. Was that
what she thought? Suddenly the answer that would have
been so clear just days ago was blurred and indistinct.
'Well?' The blue eyes were as bright as the sky overhead
and piercingly intent. 'Is it?'

'I don't know.' The words were drawn out of her in
a tiny confused whisper.

'I see.' He settled back in his seat, his face grim and
taut and the cold eyes remote and withdrawn. 'I was

right, then. I do make you nervous. Can't you forget that night eight years ago, for crying out loud?' he asked grittily as his gaze swept over her again. 'Rustle up a little of the milk of human kindness and at least try to accept what I've told you? Your antagonism is making life damn near impossible.'

'It's not what happened before...' She stopped abruptly as the handsome face turned to stone.

'Oh, charming,' he drawled coldly. 'Do I take it you just can't stand me? The present-day version, I mean?'

'Now you're just twisting what I've said,' she snapped angrily as her mind whirled in confusion. All these questions... Why couldn't he leave her alone, for goodness' sake? He was acting as though *she* were the one at fault!

'Hardly—you haven't said anything worth twisting.' His mocking contemptuous smile brought her chin jutting out and her eyes narrowing for attack. How dared he laugh at her? How *dared* he?

'Logan, if you don't like my opinion of you that's just too bad,' she said angrily, her voice low and shaking. 'But although you seem to be able to dismiss our first encounter as nothing more than youthful exuberance, I can't. I just can't, that's all. It hurt me for a long time...' She stopped abruptly, appalled at the admission she had never meant to disclose. Not to him. 'And of course it's coloured my view of you now,' she continued bravely as the silver-blue gaze remained fixed inexorably on her face. 'What on earth do you expect of me anyway?'

He opened his mouth to speak and then shut it again with a hard snap as he let his eyes run slowly over her hot face and flashing eyes. 'Melly, Melly, Melly...' His voice was suddenly thick and warm and sensual and the shiver that started at the top of her spine ran all the way down her back in a deliciously frightening trickle. 'I'll tell you one day, along with a host of other things when I know you're ready to listen.' It wasn't a threat and it wasn't a promise, more in the nature of a combination of both. 'And I *will* have you, Melly.' The shock of the words, said so softly and distinctly, brought the hairs rising on the back of her neck as though she had just heard her fate was signed and sealed. 'But only when you want me as badly as I want you.'

'Then it'll be never,' she said weakly. 'I told you, Logan, I don't go in for your sort of love games.'

'But you will.' His voice was like liquid honey. 'And believe me, Melly, my sort of love games you'll enjoy, I promise you.'

# CHAPTER SEVEN

SHE stared at him for a long time without speaking, trying to read what lay behind the warm darkness of his face, but the ice-blue eyes were obstinately remote. He was drawing her into his orbit, slowly and relentlessly, and it seemed as though she didn't know her mind from one moment to the next. Did he create this confusion, the uncertainty, on purpose? She glanced at the handsome profile as the waitress brought the toasted sandwiches. Probably. Her mouth thinned. Very probably. But then... Her innate honesty forced her brain to continue. There *was* a different side to him than she had first imagined. His home, Alexandra... He could be tender and caring.

Fool! Her mind screamed caution in the next instant. With a child maybe, but you? Let your guard down for a moment and you'll have no one to blame but yourself.

Her mind was still racing an hour later when the taxi arrived to pick them up for the airport, and all through the journey home the silent argument went on.

Logan's Lamborghini was waiting with undeniably flamboyant panache at Heathrow and as Logan opened her passenger door and she slid in he noticed the little shiver she couldn't hide. The air was a good few degrees cooler than Paris and she hadn't allowed for the change in temperature in the light cotton cardigan she was wearing over a short-sleeved summer dress.

119

'Here.' He peeled off his jumper immediately, handing it to her before moving round the car to the driver's seat and sliding in beside her.

'It's all right.' As he settled in his seat she tried to hand back the sweater which was still warm from his body and smelt faintly of his aftershave. 'Really.' The thought of immersing herself in the smell and taste of him was more than a little shocking.

'Put it on.' As she continued to hesitate he took the jumper out of her hands, lifting his arms and pulling it over her head before she could protest. As her head emerged in a ruffled gasp from the interior of the cloth she saw he was smiling sardonically. 'I'm learning with you, Amelia Higginbottom, but it's taking time.'

'Learning what?' She tried to smooth her tousled hair but could do nothing about her hot cheeks.

'To act first and ask permission later.' His voice was lazy and cool.

'I thought that was the root of all our problems?' she responded tartly as she rolled up the sleeves of the sweater a little so her hands could emerge from the depths of it. It buried her but she had to admit she felt warmer already.

'Our problems?' He turned in his seat so that he was facing her head on and she caught her breath at the sheer attractiveness of him. 'We have enough between us to share problems?' he asked softly. 'It's not all cut and dried?'

She tried to form a reply, something cool and sharp, but with the smell and feel of him all around her and the warmth from his body still seeping into hers from the soft wool she found the words wouldn't materialise. Besides which he looked so good in the dark confines of the car, so altogether, devastatingly good. Why did she have to fancy him so much? she thought suddenly. Her body really wasn't playing fair.

Once out of the airport he drove swiftly and competently along the English roads that were almost deserted at the late hour, his face sombre and dark, and his big body relaxed and easy as he controlled the powerful car. She found herself glancing under her eyelashes at the enigmatic profile more than once but could read nothing in the classical features to tell her what he was thinking.

Mere physical attraction is not the basis for any sort of relationship, she told herself firmly as they drove through the dark shadowed night. There's got to be more, much more. Friendship, genuine tenderness, an awareness of the other's needs and rights. So why, when her brain knew all that, was her body aching for his touch?

'Melly, I need to talk to you.' As he spoke into the quiet confines of the car without glancing at her, he checked in his mirror before turning off the road into a pebbled pull-in, cutting the engine and turning to look at her almost with one movement.

'What's the matter?' She stared at him nervously. Their proximity in the car normally was enough to deal with. It brought the big male body far too close for comfort and there was no way she could ignore the messages her body insisted on giving her brain. But now they had stopped things were...hot. Scorching even?

'Melly...' He stopped and shifted in his seat restlessly. 'I want us to begin again.'

'I'm sorry?' It wasn't cool. It certainly wasn't the epitome of the nineties woman, but her wide-eyed, open-mouthed stare *was* real.

'Can we just pretend that we are two people who haven't known each other very long but want to spend some time together?' he asked expressionlessly. 'The first part is true anyway.'

'Why?' She was too surprised to be tactful. 'Why, Logan?'

'As I said, I want us to begin again.' His eyes were tight on hers and how she could ever have thought of their silver-blueness as cold she didn't know. 'The past——' he shrugged big shoulders helplessly '—I can't alter it, Melly, I can't go back. I made a few mistakes when I was younger but only one I regret, because that's the one that hurt someone else badly and in a way I never intended. You weren't like the others, I knew that even then. I tried to get you to talk to me for days afterwards but you blocked me every time, and for weeks I kept tabs on you, did you know that?'

'No.' She wanted to believe him, but just how much frightened her.

'And then I left the university and circumstances changed so rapidly. I got offered a marvellous opportunity in America which I'd have been crazy not to go for.'

She remembered someone talking about that at the time, she thought silently. He'd left with a first class degree and landed the sort of chance that dreams were made of. But somehow, because it was Logan Steer, no one had been surprised.

'But I never forgot you.' She looked straight into the hard, handsome face, wishing she could read his mind as he seemed to be able to do with her so often. 'Always in the back of my mind there was a picture of England consisting of a small slim girl with hair the colour of the leaves in autumn and velvet-brown eyes. Warm eyes, eyes that a man could get used to coming home to.'

She hardly dared breathe and then, as he put out a tentative hand and traced the outline of her face with a gentle finger, she knew she was lost. The cold, hard, dynamic tycoon Logan she could just about resist, but this other one...

'I'm not asking for anything but that we take it a day at a time,' he said softly as she opened her mouth to speak, to tell him she agreed, that she'd agree to anything if only he'd keep looking at her like that. 'OK?' As she nodded silently he smiled slowly, pulling her into his arms with scant consideration for the controls of the car and kissing her until she was breathless. His mouth was demanding and sensual and the pleasure that sent the blood singing crazily through her limbs sharpened the ache in the pit of her stomach that was ever present when she was near him. As he groaned slightly, his mouth warm against her throat and his body hard against her softness, she felt an answering echo in herself that she bit back just in time. 'A day at a time.' He hadn't made any promises, hadn't spoken of anything lasting; she had to take this easy, easy and slow. But it was difficult. She would never have believed how difficult.

'Home?' He seemed to sense the mental withdrawal although her lips were still clinging hungrily to his as he moved away back into his seat, and as she nodded quietly, knowing that at that moment speech was quite beyond her, he started the powerful engine immediately.

It only took them another two or three minutes to reach the outer grounds and as they drove along the wide drive, and the house came into view she felt a moment's rushing excitement. She had to be more relaxed about all this. He had had lots of women, she knew that, but she *did* believe him when he said there was only room for one woman in his life at a time and at the moment— she shut her eyes for a split-second and then opened them wide—at the moment it was her. So she had to be cool, cool and relaxed. It was funny that that was something that came naturally around every other man but Logan...

They entered the house quietly as it was past midnight and Logan had told Mrs Sturgess, the housekeeper, in his telephone call the previous day not to wait up for them. 'A nightcap?' The words were still in his mouth as the door to the drawing-room opened with a theatrical flourish to reveal a tall, slender and very feminine shape in the doorway that Melly recognised instantly. She would have known that blonde sleek hair and beautiful cool face anywhere, *anywhere*. It had haunted her dreams for nights since she had first glimpsed it nearly three weeks ago in the photograph.

'Vanessa?' Logan's face had frozen into a blank, cold mask of surprise. 'What on earth...?'

'Darling...' The word was breathed through pouting red lips and seemed to hang in the air forever. 'I did ring this morning to see if it was OK to drop in but of course you weren't here.' The large slanted eyes, in a vivid shade of green, flickered just slightly and somehow, in that instant, Melly just *knew* that Vanessa had made this trip to see her. It was there in the iced beauty of the big eyes and the almost confrontational tilt to the blonde head. 'But dear Mrs Sturgess said you were expected late tonight with your friend...' Now the thickly lashed eyes allowed themselves to rest totally on Melly's face. 'You haven't introduced us, sweetheart...?' she drawled in an aside to Logan, who still remained motionless as though caught in a time-warp.

'I'm sorry.' He answered automatically and turned to Melly, reaching out his arm and pulling her into his side as he waved his other hand in Vanessa's direction. 'Melly, meet Vanessa. Vanessa, Melly.'

Vanessa acknowledged her with a tight smile that didn't touch the beautiful cold eyes at all. 'What a sweet name.' She sauntered across the space between them and took Logan's free arm, drawing them both towards the open drawing-room door in such a way that at the entrance Logan was forced to let go of Melly and walk through with Vanessa.

Beautifully done, Melly acknowledged silently, as she followed them into the dimly lit room. Really beautifully done. Ownership established and seniority made clear without a word being spoken.

'A drink?' Vanessa continued walking to the drinks cabinet as she indicated her own glass of what looked like white wine on a small table holding some scattered magazines. 'Logan is a brandy man, I know...' She turned and flashed a scorchingly intimate smile in his direction. 'And you'd like...?' As the smile turned to Melly it turned frosty.

'I'll see to that.' As Logan reached Vanessa's side he gently, but very firmly, took her arm and pushed her in the direction of her recently vacated seat. 'Melly, what would you like?'

'Just a tonic water, please.' What she would have really liked was to disappear to bed; the emotional turmoil of the last forty-eight hours had caught up with her and she felt deathly tired. But somehow... She caught at the impulse that had made her ask for the drink instead. Somehow it would have seemed like running away? But that was ridiculous! She raised her head as she considered the thought and caught the full force of the hard green feline gaze that was trained on her face. Or...maybe not so ridiculous.

'Dee tells me we're boarding your cat for the moment?' Vanessa said stiffly as Logan poured the drinks, her eyes drifting with hard disapproval over Logan's jumper hugging Melly's rounded curves.

We? Melly took a deep pull of air and prayed for composure. 'Yes, that's right,' she smiled carefully. 'And talking of Marmalade...?' She glanced round the room slowly, noticing the glowing embers in the massively ornate fireplace. 'He's normally hogging any sort of warmth.' She was pleased her voice sounded so relaxed and normal. Ever since she had set eyes on that undeniably strikingly beautiful face her stomach had been churning as though driven by a five-horsepower motor. Vanessa was elegant, sophisticated and very very lovely. Just Logan's type in fact.

'Oh, I shut the animals in the utility room at the back of the house,' Vanessa said airily as she lifted her glass gracefully and took a long sip of wine. 'I don't approve of animals roaming about, I'm afraid. My parents were very strict on that sort of thing when I was young, hygiene and so on, you know...' She smiled with suffocating sweetness. 'And one really must be so careful with poor little Dee. Any setback now...'

'Vanessa?' As Logan handed Melly her drink he turned back to the slim blonde, but the dark face was in severe profile and Melly couldn't see the expression on his face. 'I'd like a word, please. If you'd excuse us just a moment, Melly?'

'Oh.' Vanessa looked startled and then defensive as she followed Logan out of the room, returning in a matter of moments with a dull flush highlighting her wonderfully sculptured cheekbones. 'Such a fuss over a few animals,' she said tightly as she sat down in her seat, her eyes flashing across at Melly accusingly. 'They're fortunate to be indoors at all in my opinion.'

Her opinion obviously wasn't shared by Logan, Melly thought silently, immediately shamed by the comfort and thread of barbed satisfaction the knowledge brought.

The admonition, if there had been one, didn't seem to affect Vanessa's aplomb once Logan returned with Marmalade and Tabitha at his heels, however. The big cat was inordinately pleased to see Melly, leaping on to her lap from halfway across the room and making his pleasure at her reappearance in his life known by the almost deafening purr that reverberated from his throat in loud rhythmic waves as his paws kneaded with ecstatic concentration. She glanced up once, to share her gratification at the unusual show of feline delight, but Vanessa had leant across to murmur quietly in Logan's ear and neither of them noticed her gaze. It hurt, unbearably, to see his dark head bent to Vanessa's blonde one. And it made her angry. Very angry. And she had no right to feel like that. She knew it, but it was head knowledge not heart and there was nothing she could do about it. But in the next instant Marmalade had leapt off her lap and sauntered across to Logan, tail erect and head high.

Vanessa gave a little affected squeal at the cat's approach. 'Logan! Keep that thing away from me—you know I just loathe them.' She had been sitting on the arm of his chair but as Marmalade wound his big body against Logan's legs Vanessa moved across to her own seat with another little squeal.

If it hadn't have been ridiculous Melly would have sworn the big cat knew exactly what he was doing. Certainly the slanted eyes vied with Vanessa's for coldness as he glanced once in her direction before establishing himself at Logan's feet where he was quickly joined by the ever adoring Tabitha.

'Sorted those dogs out yet?' As Logan bent down to scratch the cat's head his voice was cool and lazy but she had seen the pleased expression on his face a second before, and it caused another strange little kick in her heart region.

Melly found the next half-hour before they retired acutely trying and it didn't change the next day. Vanessa sailed down to breakfast looking as though she had just stepped out of a London beauty salon, hair and nails immaculate, and impeccably made-up with her slim full-breasted figure encased in loose cotton trousers and a pure silk blouse that screamed a designer label. Logan was just a step behind her, whether by chance or design Melly wasn't sure, but nevertheless they entered together and the blonde's face fairly oozed satisfaction as she saw Melly in place to witness the entrance.

'Good morning.' She nodded graciously in Melly's direction, her sleek blonde hair brushing her face and a wisp of expensive perfume clouding the air. 'Did you sleep well?' It was said in the manner of a hostess enquiring after a guest's welfare and set the tone for the day. In every little thing she did and said, every word, every gesture, Vanessa managed to proclaim, with cool polite subtlety, that Logan was still very definitely hers. Dee's arrival at the breakfast-table with Mrs Sturgess was treated with sugary maternal enthusiasm that surprised Melly but which the little girl seemed almost to ignore.

And Logan? Melly glanced at him as they all left the breakfast-table, Dee having persuaded the adults to venture on a walk before lunch. How did he view

Vanessa's presence? She certainly hadn't noticed any objections.

'Mrs Sturgess, could you get Dee ready while I have a word with Melly, please?' Logan asked the efficient housekeeper as they met in the hall, and at her nod he took hold of Melly's arm and drew her towards his study opposite the drawing-room as Vanessa paused with her foot on the bottom tread of the stairs. Melly had one last glimpse of her face, taut and still, in which the narrowed green eyes gleamed like those of a witch's cat, before Logan shut the door behind them.

'I'm sorry about this, Melly.' He turned to face her, his eyes very blue and strangely guarded.

'About what?' She wanted, no, *needed*, reassurance, the reassurance of being taken into his arms and told he had really meant all he had said on the journey here, but he seemed reluctant to touch her. Was that because Vanesssa was here? Because the contrast between his beautiful ex-wife and her had hit him for the first time? Vanessa fitted into his world so well, so perfectly...

'Vanessa turning up like this.' He ran a hand through his shock of black hair and gestured irritably at the door. 'I had no idea she'd be here.'

'Does she often call in?' Melly asked carefully as she gulped away her insecurities and tried to concentrate on what he was saying. They were divorced, for goodness' sake, that had to mean something, didn't it? Didn't it?

'Now and again.' He waved an impatient hand and turned to prowl about the large room lined with books as though he found it difficult to look her in the face. 'She travels a lot—Rome, the South of France... Her parents can afford to give her anything she wants and she is their only child. They spoil her unmercifully.'

'And Dee?' She stared at his profile as he stopped to stare out of the narrow window. 'Their grandchild?'

'They've seen Dee once.' The hard voice was quite emotionless. 'They were mortified that a life that had come out of them could have had a share in producing something that was less than perfect. Vanessa has always been perfect in their eyes, you see. A beautiful baby, a beautiful child, the epitome of their success. They wanted, and made, an exquisite doll that could walk and talk as an extension of themselves.'

'Oh, Logan...' She stared appalled at the bleak outline of his face. 'They rejected Dee? How could they?'

'Oh, they could all right, and they did.' He turned to face her now and she flinched at the raw disgust and anger on his face, the skin stretched too tightly over the hard bones in a mask of pain. 'I could have killed them that night when they came to the hospital and saw Dee. The things they said...' She saw him swallow and then the harsh control was back. 'And Vanessa, she was like a sponge, soaking up their thoughts and feelings and playing them back in some sort of sick repetitive record at a time when Dee...' He stopped abruptly and shook his head as though dazed at what he had said. 'I'm sorry, Melly, I never intended to say any of this. I just wanted to explain that I've always tried to encourage Vanessa to see her child, communicate. I guess I've tried to be the antithesis of her parents to bring some balance back into the situation.'

'Yes.' She stared at him helplessly. She could see that, she *could*, but if Vanessa had been plain or ugly or even just ordinary there wouldn't be this ache in her chest at the thought of how easily the other woman just walked in and out of his life. And if she *had* been plain or ugly,

would he have been so magnanimous anyway? Did he
still love her, deep down?

'Anyway, I just wanted to explain that I had no idea
she'd be here,' he said flatly. 'The last I heard she was
in Venice with the current boyfriend.'

'She has a boyfriend?' Melly wouldn't acknowledge
that suddenly the day was brighter, the air clearer.

'One of many.' He gestured irritably. 'They come and
go like everything else in her life. But that's enough about
Vanessa...' He moved towards her and stood looking
down at her with that expression in his eyes that melted
her bones. 'Now about us——'

The knock on the door was sharp and sudden and, as
Logan uttered a muttered oath before moving away,
Melly just knew who had engineered the interruption.

'Darling, Dee is just *dying* to get started.' Vanessa
smiled gently and indicated behind her to the child who
was sitting in her wheelchair swathed in a thick blanket.

'Where's Melly?' Dee peered anxiously across the hall
into her father's face. 'She is coming, isn't she, Daddy?'

'Of course I am.' Melly brushed past Logan and
walked across to the small figure who grinned up at her
delightedly. 'And why are you wrapped up like a
Christmas parcel? It's not that cold outside. I thought
perhaps you could have a piggy-back if your Daddy can
carry such a big lump. I used to love that with my father
and it's much more fun than this old chair!'

As Vanessa started to protest Logan joined Melly at
Dee's side. 'What a good idea.' He smiled down at the
small face looking up into his so hopefully. 'Why didn't
I think of that before? We can explore that little wood
where the dogs always disappear if you like, Dee? See
what they get up to in there.'

'I don't really think that's a good idea,' Vanessa said stiffly as Dee gave an exclamation of delight. 'She's very vulnerable, Logan; she needs to be kept warm and——'

'She'll be fine.' As he spoke Logan bent down and carelessly discarded the blanket on the floor, lifting up the frail little body from the wheelchair into his arms and kissing the top of the smooth sleek head in a way that said the caress had been done many times before. 'Now, if you'll do the honours, Melly?'

As she lifted Dee from him and positioned the child on to his back Melly was horrified at the lightness of the tiny child. She was so thin, and so very delicate. Perhaps the wheelchair would have been better? But it resigned her to the status of invalid somehow, and she had wanted her to be free...

Vanessa kept up a quiet monologue of complaints through the morning, each one coated with a covering of apparent selfless consideration for her daughter. The dogs were too boisterous, even though their antics had Dee screaming with laughter. It was too cold for the child to be out, even though the October day was sunny and mild and scented with the last remnants of summer. The wheelchair was better, much safer... On this last utterance Melly had the unworthy thought, fed by the darting little glances Vanessa gave Dee's tiny arms clinging round her father's neck, that the child was getting a sight too much of Logan's attention for Vanessa's liking, but she dismissed the idea at once. Surely a mother, even one like Vanessa, couldn't be jealous of her four-year-old daughter?

Once back in the house, at Vanessa's insistence, Dee was whisked away by the housekeeper for 'a little nap before lunch' despite the child's vigorous and loud protests. 'I'm not a baby,' she objected noisily from the doorway as Mrs Sturgess prepared to carry her upstairs.

'No, but you *are* a child,' Vanessa snapped back crossly, 'and you'll do as you're told.' As Logan's head turned sharply from the glass of sherry he was pouring, Vanessa stitched a gentle but sorrowful smile on her face as she turned to Melly. 'Logan spoils her, I'm afraid,' she said with soft sweetness, 'and I do worry that she'll be too much for him.'

'Do you?' Melly had had enough erroneous fabrication for one morning. 'I think she's absolutely brilliant actually.'

'How sweet.' Vanessa's eyes turned into chips of green glass. 'And I gather you work for my... for Logan?' The hesitation had been brief, so brief that Logan, who had followed Mrs Sturgess to the door and was waving to Dee from the bottom of the stairs, hadn't caught it, but the intent was obvious. 'My husband'. She had been about to say 'my husband'. But she *wasn't* his wife any more, Melly thought with sudden savagery, and hadn't been for nearly four years.

'I work *with* him, yes.' Melly looked straight into the lovely cold eyes and prayed the sick thumping of her heart wasn't evident in her face. 'He's excellent at what he does.'

'Isn't he just?' The low throaty drawl gave the words a subtle innuendo that brought immediate heat into Melly's face. 'There's none better.' And as Vanessa turned to the tall figure who had just entered the room again, the hunger on her face was there for anyone to read. She wanted him back, Melly thought faintly, and badly. Very badly.

The rest of the day was painful, the only bright spots being the time spent with Dee, who had taken a fierce liking to her. Marmalade and the other animals were steering well clear of the house and Melly reflected that she wished she could do the same. Vanessa didn't miss an opportunity to touch or fondle Logan: the smooth white red-taloned hands were forever wandering over his face or hair or touching his arms in light intimate movements that made Melly nauseous. She literally couldn't leave him alone. How could he put up with it? she thought silently after a particularly obvious contrived incident had Vanessa sprawled momentarily against the hard masculine chest. And why? Her eyes clouded with disgust. OK, so Vanessa was Dee's mother, but he was her father, for goodness' sake, and surely he could see Vanessa's lack of interest in the child? The only time she forced herself to show any affection at all to Dee was when Logan was within earshot. Couldn't he *see* that? But maybe…? She bit her lip hard. Maybe the old saying that love was blind was working overtime? He had never really said how he felt about Vanessa, after all. Or her, for that matter. For such a physical man he was very chary with his thoughts and emotions.

At Dee's bedtime the little girl insisted that Melly read her bedtime story.

'Sorry.' Logan raised sardonic black eyebrows in Melly's direction as Mrs Sturgess relayed the child's message to the adults enjoying a drink before dinner in the large drawing-room. 'But you've made something of a hit there.'

'You don't have to apologise,' Melly said quickly as she rose swiftly, glad to escape Vanessa's cloying presence. The blonde had engineered that she sit remarkably close to Logan on the arm of his chair despite there being numerous seats scattered all across the beautiful room. 'I'd love to read to her.'

'How sweet.' As Vanessa's voice purred softly into the air the two words grated, and not for the first time that day, on Melly's nerves like sharp barbed wire. The other woman had an annoying habit of drawling them at intervals, in an elegant, patronising sort of way, if Melly said anything in the least enthusiastic about the child. 'But don't let her keep you up there all night,' the honeyed tones continued quietly. 'When you have children yourself you'll realise firmness is as necessary as kindness. Don't you think so, Logan?' She smiled gently into his face, which was wearing the remote expressionless mask it had worn all day, and Melly left before she could hear his reply. One more minute in that room and she would do something highly regrettable, she thought tightly as she climbed the stairs to Dee's room. Why she had ever come on this awful weekend she would never know!

Two of the three reasons were sitting facing her on the bed as she walked into Logan's daughter's room. Dee had her arms hugged tight round Marmalade's big soft shape as he snuggled close to her, his calm gaze portraying none of the guilt that Dee's did. 'Oh, I'm glad it's you, Melly,' Dee said quickly. 'I thought it might be Nessa.' That was another thing that Melly found most peculiar, the little girl's habit of calling her mother by her first name. 'An' I want Marmalade with me tonight; he knows when I'm sad.'

'You're sad?' Melly sat quickly on the bed, deciding to ignore the fact that she was aiding and abetting in the crime. 'Why, sweetheart?' She stroked a lock of shiny brown hair from the small forehead as she spoke. 'I'd have thought you had lots of things to be happy about today. Your Daddy's here, and your mother——'

'That's why I'm sad.' Dee looked up at her with huge brown eyes in which the devastating honesty of children was paramount. 'I always feel sad when Nessa's here. She——' the child rubbed her nose reflectively '—spoils things.'

'Dee!' Melly looked down into the little face and prayed quickly for wisdom. How on earth did one reply to something like this? 'If she does it's not because she means to.' Melly ignored the stirring of conscience and took a hard pull of air before continuing. 'It's just that she worries about you, sweetheart, she loves you and——'

'She does not.' The childish voice suddenly sounded dreadfully old. 'She thinks I ought to be in a home, but she didn't mean this one.' The small body shifted restlessly on the bed. 'But my Daddy doesn't think that; he wants me here. Nessa likes my Daddy very much, Melly, but she doesn't like me.'

'Dee...' Melly's voice trailed away as she gazed helplessly at the small face under its cap of sleek brown hair cut in an engaging little bob.

'She doesn't, Melly, an' I don't mind. Well, not much.' The big eyes were fixed tightly on her face. 'Don't you believe me?' she asked suddenly. 'Well, it *is* true. I don't tell fibs. My Grandma, the one I've never seen, was talking to Nessa on the phone once and I picked up the one downstairs to hear what they were talking about. My Grandma was saying I should be in a home, not here, and Nessa said she knew that but it wasn't her fault. An' then they talked about genes or something. I thought jeans were something you wear on your legs, Melly?'

'They are, sweetheart, they are.' Melly answered automatically as her mind raced.

'Marmalade, you're tickling me!' As Dee giggled into the cat's ginger fur the conversation swung away from Vanessa and Melly had never been more thankful for the mercurial vacillation of children. She felt angry, furiously, murderously angry, with Vanessa and her mother for their sheer cold-bloodedness and insensitivity to this tiny scrap of humanity that was battling against tremendous odds and winning hands down. How could a mother, and a grandmother, behave like that? And yet she didn't doubt Dee was telling the truth for a minute. The small child hadn't properly understood the content of the conversation she had overheard, thank goodness, but her repeating of it was too adult to be fabricated. And the pair of them thought Dee was sick? Melly bit back scalding tears angrily. The only sick ones around this place were an ice-cool blonde and her strange parents.

The next half-hour was spent in the company of Postman Pat with Marmalade doubling as Jess the cat, much to Dee's delight, and as Melly read the collection of Postman Pat stories that Dee had in her little bookcase she found herself marvelling yet again, as she had on numerous occasions throughout the day, on Dee's enormous sense of humour and zest for life despite her physical difficulties and the hours of pain she had endured in her short life.

By the time Melly was ready to leave the bedroom Dee was settled down under the covers and fast asleep. Melly sat for several minutes just watching the child as she slept, noticing the thick black eyelashes on the smooth clear cheeks, the tiny rosebud lips pursed in sleep, the small thin arms wrapped round her old teddy bear. Didn't Vanessa *see* all this? she thought painfully. Couldn't she understand how beautiful, how very courageous, her tiny daughter was? The answer was stark and clear, but how Logan had ever got involved with such a heartless, callous excuse for a woman was not, and even less comprehensible was why he continued to have any contact with her.

He *had* to love her, Melly thought painfully as she tiptoed from the little girl's room. It was the only answer that made any sense at all.

# CHAPTER EIGHT

MELLY found dinner an acutely uncomfortable affair. Her new knowledge of the extent of Vanessa's real feelings about her daughter had been the death knell to any attempt she might have made to be sociable with the cool blonde, and for the most part she sat in troubled silence watching Vanessa use every female wile in the book in a transparent attempt to woo Logan into her bed. Or to be more precise, one of *his* beds. It sickened her, it certainly disgusted her, but Logan seemed to be almost unaware of the swirling undercurrents as he sat aloof and distant at the head of the table, dark and enigmatic. She hadn't had one moment alone with him all day, Vanessa had made sure of that, even using Dee as a helpless little pawn in her game of human chess.

'You're leaving early in the morning?' Vanessa turned to her for the first time that evening.

'After breakfast.' Melly didn't even try to smile, her large brown eyes direct and cool as she stared back into the other woman's hard green gaze. 'Logan wants to say goodbye to Dee before we leave.'

'I shall leave just after breakfast too.' Vanessa turned back to Logan, who nodded non-committally. 'Things to do...'

Surprise, surprise, Melly thought grimly. And if Logan was staying another week, guess who would have been around...? 'What a shame.' As she spoke Vanessa's head swung back to meet her straight, level gaze. 'It must be something important to persuade you to leave Dee when you've only just arrived.'

As the feline eyes narrowed into green slits Vanessa's gaze ran swiftly over Melly's face and for once Melly made no effort to hide her contempt and dislike of the other woman. There was a tense, biting silence for a few seconds and, as the brown eyes didn't waver and fall, the green gaze slid on and over Melly's short curls.

'Quite.' Vanessa brushed her hair languidly from her cheek with an elegant hand on which glittered several large, and somewhat ostentatious, rings. 'But there is a bright spot on the horizon.' She reached out across the table and touched the tip of Logan's hand with a long painted nail. 'I shall be in Paris next week, darling. I'll look you up, shall I?' She turned to Melly without waiting for his reply. 'The shopping is just heavenly round Rue du Faubourg-St-Honofe and the Champs-Elysées, but of course I don't need to tell you that, do I, sweetie? You always look so chic.' She smiled with cold venom. 'Mother and I spend hours browsing.'

'I'm sure you do.' Logan's voice was cool, very cool. 'But Melly and I will be in Paris on business, Vanessa. There is no point in trying to arrange anything——'

'Oh, darling!' Vanessa made a valiant effort to be playful but the hard edge was unmistakable. 'What a fusty old killjoy you are at times! All work and no play——'

'Keeps the wolf from the door most satisfactorily,' Logan drawled drily. 'Besides which, my playtimes are more than adequate, thank you, Vanessa, although it's kind of you to be concerned. Now, who's for coffee?'

Vanessa stared at him for a long still moment, a look that Logan held with icy control, before dropping her eyes away from the piercing blueness of his with a little shrug of her slim shoulders. 'I'll have mine with a brandy, please,' she said lightly. 'Shall we go through to the drawing-room and be comfortable?' There it was again, the unmistakable hostess routine, Melly thought with something akin to disbelief as she gazed at the other woman's beautiful assured face. She really was the most brazenly complacent, unrufflable person she had ever met in her life! She would probably be a great asset to Logan in business, Melly considered with painful honesty as they left the huge table with its fine crystalware and silver cutlery. Giles, for instance, would find that air of composed self-possession immensely attractive.

The cats were established in front of the fire when they entered the drawing-room and, although the dogs skulked off when they heard Vanessa's voice, Marmalade contented himself with one scathing glance in her direction before turning back to contemplate the glowing embers. Melly had to restrain herself from clapping out loud. The cat was a match for Vanessa any day. Oh, how she wished he could talk!

'I'm sure those things are covered in fleas.' Vanessa glared with abject loathing at Marmalade's broad back as Tabitha pressed a little closer into his side. 'Look, would you say this was a flea-bite?' As she slowly drew up the hem of her dress almost to her thigh and pointed to a minute little mark at the top of one beautifully shaped silk-clad leg, Logan was spared the effort of a reply by Marmalade's sudden spin in Vanessa's direction accompanied by a loud hissing and spitting. The whole action only lasted a second or two but had the result of throwing the whole room into pandemonium out of which Vanessa emerged red-faced and shaking with anger.

'Did you see that?' She glared at Marmalade as though she would like to strangle him with her bare hands. 'It went for me, Logan. It went for me! What are you going to do about it?'

'What do you suggest I do?' Logan asked lazily. 'I should think it was the sight of all that red meat that confused the poor animal, and he only moved an inch or two, Vanessa.'

'Logan...' Vanessa's bottom lip trembled as she reached out an imploring hand only to withdraw it quickly as a warning growl erupted from Marmalade's throat. 'It doesn't like me. Get it out of here, please...' The sight of Vanessa batting her eyelashes in a little-girl-lost gesture was too much for Melly. She rose abruptly, reaching down and whisking a cat under either arm as she straightened.

'I'll put them in the study?' she asked Logan, who nodded silently, his face imperturbable. 'And then I think I'll go to bed, if you don't mind. We've got a busy day tomorrow.'

'Perhaps I do mind,' he said carefully. 'I was rather hoping for a word with you before we retired.'

'I'm sure it'll keep.' Suddenly another minute, another second, in this harem-type situation would be unbearable. In that moment she hated Logan, hated Vanessa, hated everything. She just wanted to be home, in her little flat, with Marmalade curled up in front of the small gas fire. Logan was probably enjoying this. She glared at him across the room as the thought took form. Another boost to his already oversized ego. Well, enough was enough. He could play happy families to his heart's content but not with her around, *definitely* not with her around!

She heard his voice speak her name as she left the room but didn't stop, depositing the two surprised cats in the silent study and shutting the door carefully before marching determinedly upstairs. She should never have come. She had known it! She had no excuse. Then why had she? She sat in the silence of her bedroom without switching on the light, peering into the darkness as she tried to bring her churning thoughts into order. Why *had* she come? For Marmalade? For Dee? Yes, partly, but only partly, she acknowledged after nearly an hour had crept by and she still hadn't moved. She had wanted to be with him, for whatever reason, and it had all seemed to start so well... She remembered the journey home and bit her lip hard.

Perhaps it would have been better to listen to what he wanted to say? She glanced at the closed door and shook her head slowly. She hadn't really given him a chance to explain... Explain what? She shook her head again. Well, something anyway! Something needed explaining.

After another half-hour of churning recriminations and bitter self-doubt she realised she wasn't going to get any sleep that night unless she saw Logan. Maybe he was still downstairs? She glanced at her slim neat wristwatch and saw it had just turned eleven. He was bound to still be downstairs. At the very least she could see. She needed to get a few things straight, it couldn't wait.

She left the room without a sound, walking gingerly down the large central landing from which four of the six bedrooms with their matching *en-suite* bathrooms stretched out blankly in the dim light, the wooden doors tightly shut. She peered down the large winding staircase. There were no lights on downstairs that she could see. He must have retired for the night.

She didn't know what made her turn round, very slowly, because there had been no sound to alert her to another human being's presence. Vanessa was just leaving Logan's room at the very far end of the landing and, as the other woman saw Melly, she froze for a moment in the doorway, silhouetted in the shadows like a slender ethereal spirit, her blonde hair a shining cap of pale gold and the transparent nightdress of clinging silk that she was wearing revealing every curve and indentation of her lovely body. And then she smiled. A cold, hard, satisfied twist of a smile that broke the spell that seemed to be holding Melly transfixed.

How Melly got back to her room she didn't know. Her legs were shaking so much that she wouldn't have believed they had the strength to hold her, and there was a sick buzzing in her head that sent the blood spinning crazily through her veins.

'Fool, fool, fool.' She stumbled over to the beautifully carved dressing-table and sat staring at her white reflection in the oval mirror. 'You stupid, blind fool.' She groaned deep in her chest, feeling an urge to bite and kick and scratch, to do anything to relieve the furious rage that was still mounting in a hot volcano of burning pain and fury. Again. She had let him manipulate and mould her to his will *again*. How could one woman be so incredibly stupid? *How could she*?

She was still sitting there when the knock at her door came some fifteen minutes later, and as she froze only her eyes turned towards the sound. He wouldn't. Not even Logan would do this...

'Melly?' It was his voice. 'Are you asleep? I need to talk to you just for a moment, it's important.'

Important? For a moment she considered pretending she was asleep and then the furious anger that had her stomach knotted in a giant tangle sent her marching to the door. 'Hello, Logan.' Amazingly her voice was even and controlled, betraying none of the inner agitation that turned her velvet-brown eyes black. 'What do you want?' Spell it out, she told him silently as she forced her features into a composed mask. Spell it out, you rat.

'Can I come in?' He glanced from her fully dressed figure to the room beyond.

'I don't think that's a good idea.' Something in the even neutrality of her detached cold voice must have got through to him because she saw his black brows frown for a second in quizzical thought before he nodded quietly.

'OK.' He leant against the door-frame and her heart jumped as he smiled lazily. 'You're probably right. I just wanted to explain about Vanessa in case you got the wrong idea——'

'I don't think there's any question of my getting the wrong idea, Logan.' I *saw* her come out of your room a few minutes ago, her mind screamed at him. But you don't know that, do you? And so you came along here, with your lies and sweet talk, hoping... Hoping what? That I'd fall into your bed too? Furious pride brought her chin tilting upwards and her body rigid as he nodded slowly.

'Good. Vanessa *was* my wife once, Melly—that much unfortunately is history whether I like it or not. But there's a lot more you don't know and I want to tell you——'

'But I don't want to hear it, Logan.' Now her coldness did get through to him and he straightened slowly, his eyes turning silver-blue as they took in the two bright spots of colour burning on her cheekbones. 'I don't want to hear about you and Vanessa whether it's in the past

or present. I don't care, Logan. I don't care about you
or her, and your weird, sick relationship is your own
business. But I'll tell you one thing.' And now the ice
melted as she took a step towards him. 'You both disgust
me, but perhaps you more than her. She, at least, is
honest about what she wants from you.'

'Meaning?' His face was as dark as thunder now and
he glared down at her in much the same way as she was
glaring up at him.

'Work it out.' Her lip curled as she slammed the door
so hard in his face that the whole house shook, turning
the key in the lock a second before he jerked the handle.

'Open this door, Melly.' His voice was shaking with
rage. '*Now*!'

'No.' She backed away slightly, her hand to her mouth
and her heart pounding.

'I said open it, dammit.' The handle jerked again with
furious rage. 'If I have to break it down I will.'

'You'll wake Dee up.' The child slept on the next floor
in her own small suite with the housekeeper in an adjoining room and Vanessa's rooms, when occupied,
across the landing. Melly understood from Mrs Sturgess
that Logan had moved down from the second floor to
the first some time before he and Vanessa had divorced,
and after their split had continued to let Vanessa use
their marital suite as her own rooms. There had been no
excuse for Vanessa to be on this floor, she thought
blindly, except one.

'Open it, Melly.' As she still made no move towards
the door a few tense seconds ticked by and then it opened
with the most resounding crash and Logan shot into the
room shoulder first. 'Right, what the hell is all this
about?' he ground out through tightly clenched teeth as
he came to a halt inches from her.

'As if you didn't know.' The initial shock of his entrance had been absorbed into the white-hot rage holding her body in taut stillness.

'One more smart comment, just one, and so help me I won't be responsible for my actions.' The cool debonair cynical façade that the world knew had completely disappeared and the man facing her now was gripped with such black rage that for a minute Melly panicked. 'Now, I'm asking nicely, just one more time. What is this about?'

Melly stared at him, her throat dry with fear and her heart pounding so hard it hurt. She couldn't have been wrong, could she? But no, of course not. She had *seen* Vanessa and the cool blonde had been all but naked. And the whole day had been a lead-up to the night, all the gestures and touching and silly little giggles the other woman was so good at. Damn him, what did he take her for? Maybe his other women would put up with whatever he dished out but she had *seen* Vanessa throw herself at him all day and he hadn't done a thing to stop her.

'It's about Vanessa leaving your room a few minutes ago,' she said shakily. 'As if you didn't know. I don't know what you think you are playing at, Logan, but I've had enough.'

'Enough?' His face had frozen into an icy mask in which the only live things were his eyes, piercingly cold and as sharp as glass. 'So Vanessa came to my room. And what? We made love? Is that it?'

'She was in her nightdress.' Suddenly the urge to burst into tears was so strong that she forced her voice a shade higher and tighter to combat the weakness.

'I don't care if she was stark naked,' he said grimly, his eyes glittering in the darkness of his face. 'So you saw Vanessa leave my room and immediately assumed she'd also been in my bed? In spite of all I've told you, all I've said, you didn't even see fit to ask me about it before you jumped to your erroneous conclusion?' Strangely as he talked the anger was leaving his face to be replaced by a stark weariness, almost a contempt. 'I told you how I felt on the way here, and yet you thought I'd jump at the chance to have a woman, any woman, like a dog after a bitch in heat?' The cruel crudity jarred her bones and froze her tongue. 'Well, I've had enough too, more than enough. I've never allowed a woman to get away with half of what you have and I sure as hell don't intend to apologise for what I am one more time. Damn your narrow, closed, suspicious little mind, Melly, and you can think what you like. About Vanessa, about tonight, about me!'

He turned and left in one furious movement although this time the door closed with studied softness behind him. And that, more than anything else, brought home the fact that he had meant what he said. The control was back, the cool, icy control with which he ran his life, and it was in that frame of mind he had finished with her for good. What had she done? As she sank on to the thick wool carpet her mind felt as though it was going to explode. Had she been wrong? Misread things? Fallen into a carefully prepared trap that Vanessa had woven like a big black spider?

The night crept by, each minute painfully long, and by the time the first tentative streaks of dawn were colouring the charcoal sky a dull mauve she still hadn't closed her eyes. She rose stiffly from the bed where she had been lying, still fully clothed, and walked wearily into the adjoining bathroom, stripping off her clothes and standing for a full ten minutes under the shower as she let the warm water wash away all the dried tears from her face and bathe her clean, at least on the outside. Inside she felt wretched and desperate, grimy with self-doubt and discouragement.

After washing her hair and drying it into soft curls that framed her pale face in shining chestnut, she applied careful make-up to disguise the ravages of a sleepless night and dressed slowly in the pencil-slim skirt and pale gold blouse she had laid out the night before. She surveyed herself in the mirror as she finished. Every inch the cool, collected career-woman...if one didn't look too closely, that was. And was that what she wanted from life? A sparkling career, with all the advantages such dedication assured: a beautiful flat, lovely clothes, the ability to travel and please herself? Did she? She stared back at the wide-eyed reflection in the mirror silently. She had been so sure of the answer once, but now... Now everything was in ashes.

'Good morning.' Logan was alone as she entered the breakfast-room, and raised his eyes briefly from the newspaper before returning to his coffee. The blank emptiness of the expression on the dark features was like a slap on the face, but she forced herself to answer in the same cool tone he had used and poured herself a cup of coffee without further comment.

'We will need to leave within half an hour. If you would like to say goodbye to Dee, she is in her room with Marmalade and Tabitha.' As he spoke he rose from the table and nodded briefly in her direction before striding quickly from the room. She gazed after him as a sick dullness reached out to engulf her. He couldn't make it more clear that her presence was distasteful to him. Well, she hadn't asked to come on this trip when all was said and done!

'There you are.' Mrs Sturgess smiled cheerfully as she entered the room with a fresh rackful of toast. 'Would you like a cooked breakfast this morning, dear?'

'No, thank you, the toast is fine,' Melly said quickly. The thought of eating anything at all was nauseating. 'Isn't Vanessa up yet?' she asked carefully as the little woman busied herself clearing Logan's empty plates.

'Miss Reiser left late last night apparently,' Mrs Sturgess said briefly, her tone expressing extreme disapproval. 'I expected her to say goodbye to the child, but there you are.' She suddenly looked straight at Melly, her round honest face open and forthright. 'It's none of my business of course, but why she bothers to come here at all I shall never know. She couldn't wait to change back to her maiden name once the divorce came through, as though that would wipe the little one's existence off the planet. Mind you, I think she's regretted it since, but not on account of the child if you get my meaning.' Melly stared at her without speaking, unsure of how much to say. 'Thought she could swan off when the going was tough and breeze back in when things were easy again.' The round bright eyes bored into Melly's brain. 'But then, he's never invited another woman here before, so I think madam got something of a gliff.'

'I'm only here because of the cat,' Melly said weakly as her heart started thumping.

'Is that so?' Mrs Sturgess nodded quietly. 'Well, be that as it may...' She nodded again as her gaze swept over Melly's face. 'Mr Logan is not what he seems, you know, not at all. I've worked for him for five years now, lived in for the last four, and I can tell you there isn't a finer man. I'd rather have a hard shell and a soft centre any day than the other way round.' She subjected Melly to one more lightning glance before bustling out of the room in her usual sprightly fashion, shutting the door carefully behind her with another sharp little bounce of her head.

And what did all that mean? Melly sat with the coffee-cup half raised to her lips for long seconds before replacing it in the saucer untouched. It was strange that Vanessa had left so suddenly like that, but then if she thought about it she had found most things about Vanessa somewhat abnormal. Melly bit her lip as she let her gaze move round the room one last time. She'd probably only come back here to pick up Marmalade and that wouldn't necessitate her stopping at all. And then Logan would be out of her life for good. She closed her eyes briefly at the sharp little pain in her heart region and then shook her head angrily. She'd have to pull herself together and *fast*—this was pathetic.

Goodbyes over, the journey to the airport was conducted in an icy silence that forbade any sort of conversation and lasted through the brief flight to Paris and beyond. Once back at the hotel Logan saw her to her room, deposited her case just inside the door and left after a cursory nod, his face dark and withdrawn.

She stared after him for a second before shutting the door slowly. Why, after all that had happened, when he had rent her heart apart for the second time, did she still find him so attractive? What was this sensual, almost violent fascination that she felt in his presence, even when she was consumed with rage or hurt or just sheer weariness as now? 'It's animal lust.' She spoke out loud into the empty room as she slowly began to unpack. 'Dangerous and risky and not to be messed about with.' But she couldn't think any more. Her head was aching, her eyes throbbing, and she had a full day's work ahead

of her. Which was probably just as well. Thinking did
no good at all around Logan. From now on it was a
luxury definitely *not* to be indulged in. The gulf was
wider than it had ever been and there was no way to
cross it even if she wanted to, and the bottom line was
still there, still waiting... Vanessa.

The next few days were easier than Melly had expected,
mainly because of Logan's prolonged absences. He made
one or two appearances for a few minutes each day but
most of the time appeared to be working directly on site.
Giles had purchased a magnificent old building almost
at the centre of Paris in the old market area of Les Halles
which was one of the city's most vibrant entertainment
areas day and night, and in usual Giles fashion, now the
formalities had been completed, was anxious to push on
as fast as he could. The evenings were tense, as they all
shared a table in the hotel's restaurant, but the presence
of the others helped to ease any difficult moments and
as long as Melly remembered to keep her eyes away from
the tall, sardonic, dark figure opposite her she managed
to eat enough for things to appear normal.

And it was in the evening, on the tenth day of their
return to Paris, that Vanessa made her appearance. She
had known that the other woman had phoned him the
day after they had got back because she had been with
the others downstairs, enjoying a pre-dinner drink, when
the call had come through, but Logan had had it trans-
ferred to his room so she had no idea what had transpired or whether he was seeing Vanessa or even if the
other woman was in Paris. But now she strolled into the
small cocktail bar, green eyes gleaming.

'Logan, darling...' The beautiful blonde was dressed
to kill in a tight little number in red velvet that hugged

her slim shape in all the right places, and the young man she had in tow looked distinctly uneasy as she waved a slender red-tipped hand in their direction. 'We thought we'd try here for a meal this evening. If it's good enough for my ex, it's got to be good.' She laughed throatily and Giles's eyes sparked with interest.

'I don't think I've had the pleasure...' He glanced expectantly at Logan, who moved lazily off the stool he was occupying and walked across to Vanessa's side, drawing her and the young man, who looked distinctly reassured at Logan's bland face, towards their small group. Introductions completed, he sat back in his seat, calm and composed and dark face enigmatically aloof, watching the others through half-closed, narrowed eyes as he drank another cocktail.

Melly found her gaze straying to him more than once as he watched Vanessa charming Giles, and on one occasion, as the piercing silver eyes suddenly fastened on her wide brown ones, he raised sardonically cruel black eyebrows in cynical mockery of them all. What was he thinking? she asked herself weakly. There was no way of telling. But Giles was well and truly smitten. She saw his square blunt face flush as Vanessa lightly tapped his arm in some flirtatious repartee. In fact all the men were hanging on Vanessa's every word, their laughter loud and raucous, except one... And that was the one this was all for, Melly thought grimly. Did she love him? Did *he* love her? What was this bond that held him to her when most men would have cut loose? But then, probably he didn't want to. Perhaps an open relationship like the one it appeared he shared with Vanessa was what he wanted.

'How long are you in Paris?' Giles asked Vanessa after a few minutes, his face moist and his lips wet. 'I've or-

ganised a little treat for us all at the end of the week.'
He mentioned a well-known nightclub that was both expensive and exclusive. 'A reward for jobs well done, but
I'm sure everyone would be only too pleased for you to
come along.' He was speaking specifically to Vanessa
and, as the young man at her side shifted uncomfortably, Melly felt a sudden distaste for it all.

'Have you been to Paris before?' As she bent forward
and engaged the youth in conversation he seemed to de-
flate with relief; he had clearly been feeling out of his
depth and his pleasant young face became animated and
relaxed as they chatted. She was laughing at some non-
sense he had said as the group moved to go into dinner,
and as she raised her head she suddenly met a blindingly
fierce blue gaze that robbed her of breath and almost
caused her to miss her step.

'Careful.' Logan moved forward instantly, his eyes still
hard. 'We don't want you to hurt yourself, do we?' He
took her arm in a grip that was punishing, moving her
round his body so that he effectively cut off the others
and ushering her to her seat without relaxing his hold
an iota. The only way she could have released herself
was to cause a scene so she suffered the indignity in
silence, glaring at him as they sat down and then stead-
fastly refusing to glance in his direction all through the
meal. What had all that been about?

Vanessa and Alan, her escort, were sitting some way
across the room for which she was thankful, and she
noticed, with a little shred of wry amusement, that Giles
couldn't take his eyes off the other woman all night,
leaping up the instant the meal was finished to ask the
other two to join them for coffee in the bar which
Vanessa immediately agreed to.

She couldn't quite gauge Vanessa's treatment of
herself. The other woman had totally ignored her
presence as far as she could, but when the green eyes
touched her face she could feel the malignant touch at
once. As they all walked through for coffee Melly
noticed, with a little dart of sympathy, that Alan contrived to sit at her side. This had been a rotten evening
for him, she thought understandingly as they began to
talk again, Vanessa being occupied with Giles. He must
be feeling more than a little humiliated. Because of that
she concentrated on trying to make him feel comfortable,
besides which it gave her an excuse not to have to look
at Logan and Vanessa. Any glance, any contact at all
between them, seemed to cut through her like a knife.

'Well, we really must go, darlings...' As Vanessa rose
gracefully to her feet after an hour Melly bit back a sigh
of relief. Alan had been getting a little too friendly,
probably due to the drink, and in the last few minutes
she had been vitally aware of a dark face watching her
every move, two blue eyes burning into the back of her
head even when her face was turned. 'Come along,
sweetie-pie.' Vanessa crooked a languid finger in Alan's
direction in much the same way one would summon a
playful puppy and, as the young man's face flushed a
dark red, Melly gave his hand a little squeeze.

'It's been nice meeting you.' She smiled goodbye into
the dark blue eyes.

'Are you sure you're not free for dinner?' he asked
in a low undertone that couldn't reach the others' ears.

'Quite sure.' She smiled dismissively. 'I'm a working
girl, remember.'

As they all walked into the hotel lobby Melly took the
opportunity to disappear into the lift as the others said
their farewells to Vanessa. She had had enough hypocrisy

for one evening, more than enough. As the lift stopped
on her floor she heard the one further down the corridor
whir to a halt but the sound didn't connect, and she had
just inserted the key in the lock and opened the door,
kicking her shoes off as she walked through the doorway
with a thankful sigh, as a human thunderbolt exploded
into the room along side of her.

'Logan!' She thought she had seen him angry before
but nothing, nothing had prepared her for the black rage
that seemed to consume each feature of his face into a
dark devil's mask.

'Are you seeing him again?'

'What?' The sound of his voice had been chilling, the
words snarled through clenched teeth.

'I said are you seeing him again, the little boy wonder?'
As he slammed the door shut with the back of his foot
she flinched from the darkness on his face. 'Don't you
know what sort of man he is? A gigolo, the sort of pretty
boy that older women hire to be seen about with?'

'What are you talking about?' she whispered faintly.

'And you dared to criticise my morals?' He grasped
her arms and shook her hard, his eyes burning with a
deadly fire. 'When all the time you were prepared to
encourage someone like him?'

'You've got this all wrong——'

But he never heard her because in the next instant his
mouth had riveted on to hers in a kiss that was more
violent than she would ever have dreamt possible, his
arms crushing her to him in an agony of rage as he plun-
dered her inner mouth, his breathing harsh and ragged,
immobilising her wrists behind her back with hard male
strength. As she started to struggle she realised he was
holding her in such a way that every movement brought
their bodies into more intimate contact, her softness

captivated by his rigid masculine thighs and her breasts brushing against his chest in stimulating helplessness.

'If you want someone to make love to you it will be me,' he ground out furiously against her mouth. 'Not some callow youth who sells his wares in the marketplace. Do you hear me? *Do you hear me?*'

But he had taken her mouth again and she couldn't reply and she realised she was frightened, desperately, helplessly frightened, but as much by the raging, overpowering need that was sending spirals of desire shooting through her limbs as by his dangerous rage. The taste, the smell of him was all around her and she had been resisting it for so long.

As her heated blood surged through her veins the sensation of being held by him, so close that she could hear the thudding of his heart through her own skin, vied with the knowledge that she couldn't, *mustn't* lower her defences and succumb to his mastery. He moved her hands into one of his, still behind her back, and as the other roved over her shaking body she felt the rich swell of one breast caressed briefly in its flight, the peak immediately blossoming to his touch.

She had to fight him. It was the only thought that she remembered as her body betrayed her. *She had to*: she loved him too much to be just another of his passing fancies eventually left by the wayside of his busy life.

Loved him? The shock of recognition froze every nerve and sinew. But of course she did. She had been fighting against the knowledge in her head for weeks even as her body and emotions had been telling her the truth from day one. She loved him. She had always loved him. She would die loving him.

She hadn't known she was crying until the pressure of his mouth suddenly lifted, his eyes tight on her face as his own turned white. 'Melly?' He was still holding her close but as he peered down and saw her wet cheeks, the tears still seeping through her closed lashes in silver rivulets, he moved back a pace, releasing her body from his. 'Melly, look at me.' But she couldn't. She stood, swaying slightly in her overwhelming grief, rent through with the knowledge that her love for him meant a lifetime of loneliness. And she didn't *want* to be alone but until this moment she hadn't realised how much her own mate, children, a home where love reigned, had featured in the dark subconscious of her mind.

'Go away.' And still her eyes were closed, weighted down with a thousand images that were unbearable. 'Just go away. I hate you.'

And then she was standing alone in the empty room as he left without another word. Utterly alone.

# CHAPTER NINE

THE vacuum that reached out to suck her into its empty void held over the next few days and she was glad. Glad that all feeling seemed to have left her and that she was merely a hollow shell working on automatic, untouchable, bare of emotion, dead. She didn't think she could have lived feeling as she had the first few minutes after Logan had left before the vacuous blankness took over.

And it was in this state of mind that she got ready for the evening out at the nightclub that Giles had arranged. When it was first mentioned that Vanessa might join them she had contemplated producing a headache on the night but now, strangely, that didn't seem necessary. Because it didn't matter. Nothing mattered.

She dressed mechanically in the little cocktail dress she had bought before she left England to supplement her evening clothes. It was beautifully cut in white satin, short, with tiny strap sleeves over her shoulders and a low rolled neck that set off the simple design admirably, as well as being a perfect foil for the smooth creamy hue of her skin and deep red hair. When she was ready she glanced, almost without interest, into the full-length mirror. The dark grey eyeshadow she was wearing made her eyes look huge in the smooth skin of her face, but their expression caught and held her for a moment as she gazed at the pale reflection. They were the eyes of a wounded doe, not a person, and as she felt a flash of pain sear through her chest she groaned aloud in protest.

She didn't want to feel again, to have to cope with the pain that would bring. This blessed anaesthetising numbness had allowed her to look at Logan over the last few days without crumbling, to take his cold veiled eyes and hard grim face in her stride. She couldn't begin to feel again, and not tonight when she needed more than anything to be strong.

She hauled her lipstick out of the matching evening bag quickly, applying it to the pink skin of her lips before adding a little blusher to her pale cheeks. That was better. She looked again in the mirror, her eyes veiled. Much better. She would get through this. She *would*.

She left her room quietly, praying that by some mischance Logan wouldn't appear in the corridor, but there was no sign of him, either in the lift or in the small cocktail bar downstairs where they had all arranged to meet. The others were all there, including Vanessa, and for a second as Melly's eyes rested on the beautiful blonde all other thoughts slid right out of her mind. The other woman was wearing a dress fashioned in black lace, thin black lace, and the smooth pale skin of her body shone through the dark material in what was almost indecent exposure. The dress was pencil-slim to the floor and cut away at both sides to the thighs, the strapless bodice plunging to meet it in a sharp V that ended well below the navel. It was daring, incredibly sensual, overpoweringly erotic, and Giles was practically drooling as he hung over Vanessa's bar stool, his face scarlet and his eyes popping out of his head.

'There you are...' Vanessa glanced up as Melly joined them, her green eyes cold and calculating as they ran over Melly's slender body in the white satin, and her thin, beautifully shaped mouth pursed in a small smile of satisfaction. 'You look so...sweet.'

'Thank you.' Melly found the numbness was disappearing fast. 'You...' She hesitated, lost for words in the face of Vanessa's amazing semi-nakedness.

'Don't,' Logan finished for her from behind. Melly forced herself to show no reaction to his presence although the deep dark voice brought immediate heat to her limbs. 'Sweet is not an adequate description to fit your dress, Vanessa,' he continued blandly. 'Is it legal?'

'Of course, darling.' Melly couldn't see Logan's face as he was still standing just behind her, but Vanessa seemed less than pleased at his sardonic response to her appearance, the feline eyes narrowing slightly as she watched him. 'And I'm glad you like it.'

'Are you?' Logan's voice sounded mockingly amused at the assumption.

'And you look wonderful,' Vanessa continued lightly as though he hadn't spoken. 'But then you always do, with or without clothes.' She had spoken the last words softly, in a slow purring kind of voice that wouldn't have reached the others' ears but was certainly intended for Melly's.

'You still have a way with words.' Logan's voice was cool and dry and then he moved infinitesimally closer so that the hard outline of his body touched Melly's and she ceased to think about anything but the effect his closeness was having on her overloaded senses.

'Try this cocktail, Melly,' he said softly in her ear. Somehow her fingers managed to wind round the thin stem of the big fluted glass and make a reasonable attempt to transport it to her mouth as he placed it carefully in her hand, his arm reaching round her from behind. 'Do you like it?' As he spoke he turned her slightly so that she was facing him at a side angle and as she looked at him, really looked at him for the first time for days, her legs almost buckled.

He looked tired. Devastatingly handsome as usual, undeniably gorgeous in the dark dinner-jacket and snowy white shirt that threw the blackness of his hair into stunning contrast, but still . . . tired. As though he hadn't slept for nights.

'I said, do you like it?' He indicated the drink in her hand and she glanced down almost vacantly.

'I think so.' She took a deep breath and prayed for composure. This really wouldn't do. 'Yes, yes, thank you, it's lovely.'

'Good.' He smiled slowly and, as Giles claimed his attention, Melly's gaze wandered upwards, to be transfixed in mid-air by the sheer malignant force of Vanessa's. For a split-second the green eyes were black with hate and then, as Melly blinked, Vanessa glanced away quickly, turning to make conversation with Alfred Hynes on the left of her.

Had she imagined it? Melly asked herself as she stood stock-still before taking a large gulp from her glass. No. As the pink liquid sent a warm glow down her throat she knew she hadn't mistaken that loathing. For some reason Vanessa was jealous of her, crazily jealous, but why? Surely the beautiful blonde knew she had all the cards stacked in her favour? How could Melly compete with her? The dress said it all.

By the time they got to the nightclub Melly had found the headache she had planned had become a definite reality. The combination of hardly any food all day, sleepless nights and the dangerous emotion that seemed to be sweeping in great waves under the surface and all around them had produced a sick thudding at the back of her eyes. As they joined the rest of the party, several

French officials that Giles had made it his business to
know along with their wives, she tried to concentrate
very hard on maintaining a calm 'secretarial' image, but
it was difficult when Logan engineered that she sit at his
side and the scent of his aftershave was doing crazy things
to her equilibrium. She despised herself that she could
melt like this, especially when she *knew* he valued her
so little, that it was all a game, but it was something
over which she had no control.

'Come on, sweetie-pie.' They had just finished eating
when Vanessa leant across from her seat next to Giles
and tapped Logan's arm invitingly. 'Show me you still
know how to dance as well as in the old days.' There
was a wild note in the other woman's voice now, a hostile
bid for attention that manifested itself in the shrill tone
and high-pitched laughter that had increased steadily with
each drink. 'I mean it, Logan, I want to dance.'

'Of course.' Logan rose to his feet in one smooth
movement but Melly noticed that his eyes were that pure
silver-blue that meant he wasn't amused and, as he led
Vanessa on to the large dance-floor to join the other
couples moving slowly to the live band, the big body was
taut and straight as though avoiding anything but the
most necessary contact with the voluptuous and near-
naked body at his side.

But they looked good together. Melly couldn't drag
her eyes away from the big masculine body, so dark and
tall, and the slender sensual blonde pressing into his
thighs at every opportunity. 'Some woman, eh?' Giles
moved to Logan's vacant seat, his eyes hungry as they
followed the couple's progress round the floor. 'If anyone
was going to put a ring through my nose it'd be
that one.'

'Not the most romantic way of expressing yourself, Giles.' Melly smiled with what she hoped was calm composure. 'You like her, then?'

'Too true.' Giles looked her straight in the face for a moment. 'More than like. I've asked her to come to Shaolake for the weekend when we get back to England and she's thinking about it.' Shaolake was Giles's palatial home in the heart of Harlow. 'But what I want to know is...' He hesitated and Melly was amazed to see her boss stumbling for words. 'Is she still...attached to Logan? What I mean is...' He stopped again. 'I've got no illusions about the woman, Melly. She's a hard piece but I like 'em like that. Can stand up for herself, knows what she wants. But——' he rubbed the end of his nose '——how do things stand between the pair of 'em?'

'I've no idea, Giles.' I can't stand this, Melly thought wildly, the world's gone mad. 'Why don't you ask her?'

'Because I don't think I'd like the answer,' Giles said grimly. 'Seems to me she's still got the hots for Logan, know what I mean?'

Oh, I know what you mean, all right, Melly thought painfully. I know exactly what you *mean*, Giles! So even Giles, who was not the most sensitive of creatures, could clearly see that there was still something between Logan and his ex-wife? 'If you want to know where you stand, ask Vanessa,' Melly said quietly as she shifted in her seat, watching Logan and Vanessa wind their way back to the table. The other woman's face was not smiling and the green eyes were narrowed, hardening still more as they rested on Melly's face for a moment before moving on to Giles. 'Or maybe Logan?' She glanced at Giles for a moment.

'Oh, very funny.' He gave her one of his superior frowns. 'Logan is not the sort of man you question about his love-life, Melly—not unless you've got a death wish, that is.' He moved back into his original seat as the others reached them.

Melly danced several times before the Parisian floor-show, a dazzling spectacle of lovely young dancers performing a very energetic cancan, but not with Logan. Two of the French contingent asked her, Giles asked her, even old Alfred took a turn round the floor, but Logan sat back in his chair seemingly quite relaxed, his eyes lazy and amused and his big body almost separate from them all. And she had never been more vitally aware of him. All through the floor-show Vanessa flirted quite outrageously, first with Giles, who gave the impression of not being able to believe his luck, then with Logan who eyed her with a dry cynicism that would have withered a lesser creature, but although he seemed to find the blonde's attempts to be seductive amusing rather than sexy, Melly did not. She found her temper was on the boil again, the numbness of the last few days evaporating into the air. But compounded in what she had thought was mere rage in the past she now recognised other, more subtle emotions. A sharp, acrid jealousy for a start, painful bitterness against fate, resentment, an aching loss... And she didn't want to *think* like this, *be* like this. She barely saw the dancers as they shrieked for the last time and ran squealing off the stage. She loved him and she hated him for what he was turning her into.

'Melly?' As she came out of her black thoughts she saw that Logan had risen and extended his hand, obviously waiting for her to join him on the dance-floor. And now there was nothing lazy or amused about the emotion darkening his narrowed eyes and she realised, with a little jolt, that he had been playing a part all evening. There was something burning beneath that cool exterior, something red-hot and dangerous, and for a moment she contemplated refusing the outstretched hand. But that would be cruel and humiliating and she found, in spite of his treatment of her, that she just couldn't do that to him in front of all the assembled company.

She found herself trembling as they reached the dance-floor and, as he took her into his arms, holding her close around her waist so she was forced to raise her hands to his shoulders, the shaking increased. She had to be cool, cool and composed, had to forget that this was Logan... But it was no good. As she gazed up into his darkly handsome face, at the piercingly intent eyes and hard sensual mouth, she tried desperately to maintain a bland, offhand demeanour but it was wafer-thin, and somehow, when he looked at her, she suspected he knew it.

'You are breathtakingly lovely.' His voice was soft and deep and husky and stirred her very bones. 'Too lovely to be real.' She tried to smile but it was hopeless. His skin was clear and darkly bronzed, his eyes a piercing blue and his hair, black as midnight and touched with silver at his temples, crowned the sensual attractiveness that was an essential part of this man. There was something in the high male cheekbones and dominant aquiline nose that was almost savage, reflected again in the hard pitiless mouth. He would eat her up and spit her out without even noticing, she thought dazedly. Probably her only worthwhile attribute to a man of the world like him was her innocence? She was a novelty, a new toy, something to balance the wild sensuality of women like Vanessa who offered him their all every day of the week? But when the challenge was no more, when the desire had been sated...?

'Logan...' She tried to move away within the circle of his arms but he merely drew her closer and it felt so good, as though it was where she belonged.

'Relax.' Her head was resting against his broad chest now, his chin resting in the red silk of her hair. 'You're quite safe. Not even the big bad wolf would dream of having his wicked way in front of such an elegant audience.' And the mockery hurt, badly.

'This is just a game to you, isn't it?' she stated flatly, moving away from him so sharply that he was surprised into letting her go. 'Well, go and play with someone else.' And she left him standing in the middle of the dance-floor as she surprised him again for the second time in thirty seconds, walking through the throng of dancers and past the crowded tables out through a small side door and into a dark little courtyard stacked with crates and boxes.

She had sensed he was following her and as she swung round in the middle of the small space he was there behind her, his face indistinct in the thick shadows. 'What the hell is the matter with you?' he asked furiously. 'I mean *just* what is it that makes you tick?'

'What makes me tick?' Over the last few days she had felt she would never experience real emotion again but she had been wrong: it was throbbing through her veins now, hot and viciously fierce. 'Well, let's just start with what doesn't make me tick, shall we? The sight of Vanessa almost naked doesn't do a lot for me actually, neither does the fact that she's been hanging over you like some sort of sick leech all night. But then she is Alexandra's mother? *Her mother*!' The last two words were an explosion of violent disgust. 'She doesn't know the meaning of the word. Your wife——'

'My ex-wife.' His voice broke into her raging tirade like drops of iced water. 'Vanessa is my ex-wife, Melly.'

'Oh, so you've noticed that?' She glared at him, a small pale figure in the white dress in the dark of the night. 'I'm amazed.'

'You're amazed?' Now he was at her side, his eyes glittering. 'I doubt it. I doubt if anything I do or say could possibly amaze you. Your opinion of me is so low it couldn't get any lower.'

'That's right.' She barely knew what she was saying now, the frustrated love and deep hurt making her almost incoherent with pain. 'But when your *ex*-wife still uses your home as her own, when she feels her entry into your bedroom is her right——'

'Not any more.' In contrast to her shaking voice his was low and deep. 'She doesn't have unlimited access to my home any more and she hasn't been in my bed for nearly five years.'

'I don't believe you!' She spat the words into his face.

'Then that is your right.' As she went to move past him he caught her arm, forcing her to stop. 'But you aren't going to walk out on me without hearing the facts, Melly. This time you *will* hear them. If I have to gag you and tie you up you will damn well listen.'

'You wouldn't dare——'

'Try me.' He shook her slightly as he spoke. 'You are going to listen to me now, listen until I'm finished. I'd planned to do this some time in the future, somewhere more comfortable and infinitely more conducive to breaking through that steel-clad mind of yours, but this will have to do.'

'Logan, I'm warning you——'

'And I'm warning you,' he said roughly. 'I'm sick of other people causing problems between us. I've tried a

softly-softly approach since that fiasco at the hotel—
hell, since the first time we met again I've walked on
eggshells, but I've had enough. You are going to hear
the truth now whether you like it or not, and then it's
damn well up to you what you do with it.'

'I know the truth.' She tried to shrug his hands off
her arms but they were made of iron.

'The hell you do.' He stared down into her white face,
his eyes brilliant in the darkness like a big black cat of
the night. 'The hell you do,' he repeated softly. 'The
truth is that I love you, that I've loved you since the
first night I met you when you were nineteen and scared
to death of boys and I was a brash twenty-three-year-
old who went too fast, too soon.'

'That's crazy.' She tried desperately to break free of
his hold. 'You left the country, married Vanessa——'

'And I frightened you off so badly you wouldn't have
anything to do with me,' he continued huskily as though
she hadn't spoken. 'I tried and tried and then decided
I'd give you a breathing space, get away for a while until
you finished university and then I'd be waiting for you
when you'd had time to sort out how you really felt.'

'I don't believe you, Logan.' This time she managed
to wrench free from his hands and stood trembling in
front of him, her eyes enormous. 'You slept with
Vanessa, you *married* her——'

'I'm a man, not a monk, Melly.' He didn't attempt
to touch her again and she made no attempt to move
away. 'It might not be gallant, but Vanessa threw herself
at me and I needed a woman, it was as simple as that.
I hadn't touched a female since that night with you and
I was burning up inside. She was there, she was available
and more than willing and apparently quite prepared to
treat it all as some sort of pleasant interlude with no ties

or involvement. And I fell for it.' He ground his teeth, the sound violent in the stillness of the velvet darkness. 'And I probably got exactly what I'd asked for. The next thing, she was pregnant. I'd slept with her twice, *twice*, and after the second time I felt so nauseated with myself I'd ended the relationship but——' he sighed harshly '—fate has a way of making us pay for our mistakes. So I married her, yes.'

'And then Dee was born,' Melly said grimly.

'Then Dee was born.' He eyed her quietly. 'And what I'm going to tell you now I've never told another living soul. When Vanessa first saw Dee she wanted to have her taken away, adopted, put in a home, anything... That was before her parents came on the scene and added their lament. I tried to talk her round but it got to the stage where I dared not leave her alone with the baby in case...' He stopped abruptly. 'Well, I didn't leave her alone with Dee. That's when Mrs Sturgess took over. Vanessa left after four months. She said the sight of Dee was making her ill and by that time I was glad to see her go. And then when Dee was six months old she had a kidney operation to save her life and I discovered...' He stopped again, turning from her in the dim light and standing so that just the profile of his face was facing her. 'I discovered I couldn't be her father.'

'What?' Melly felt as though the world had stopped spinning and she was floating in some strange alien space. 'I don't understand?'

'Neither did I.' He laughed harshly, the sound rasping against her ears. 'It was her blood, you see, Dee's blood. It showed conclusively that no way could she be related to me. And when I got hold of Vanessa she was almost casual about it all. The real father wasn't wealthy—some one-night stand she'd picked up in a bar somewhere.

And then it all came out. I'd known I wasn't the first, of course, but it appeared I wasn't even the twenty-first; but I *was* rich, I'd been in the right place at the wrong time and she liked my technique in bed.' He eyed her bitterly, his face dark and cynical. 'Hoist with my own petard, as they say.'

'But if Dee isn't your child...?' She stopped helplessly. 'I don't understand.'

'She is mine in everything but the biological sense,' he said fiercely. 'I was there just after she was born, I held her through the first long nights when she was in pain and couldn't sleep, I saw her first smile. It was my hand she reached out to when she first became aware of other people...' He stopped abruptly. 'And I could give her the chances she needed to get well, whatever money could buy, as well as providing a safe secure home and a family environment. The doctors had warned me she was going to have to face operation after operation and that her mental stability could make or break the physical healing. But all that aside——' he shrugged slowly '—I had six months of bonding. I loved her.'

'And Vanessa?' She felt she was losing her grip on reality but she believed him. No one would lie about something like this.

'Vanessa is Dee's only real parent,' he said flatly, 'in the natural sense. I felt that was important somehow. I suppose I felt morally obliged not to cut Dee off from her. I don't feel like that now, not lately. I could only be doing Dee a favour if I stopped Vanessa ever setting eyes on her again, but of course that is impossible. But I've told Vanessa that she keeps to the visiting rights now and everything has to be set on a more formal footing. I thought by keeping the door open I could perhaps influence their getting to know each other, perhaps encourage a bond of some sort. Other women learn to love their children in spite of problems.'

'But Vanessa?' Melly asked incredulously. Surely anyone could see that Vanessa's decision to stay in Logan's life had nothing to do with a four-year-old child, albeit her own daughter, and everything to do with a thirty-two-year-old man with eyes the colour of blue ice and a smile women would kill for? He must be able to see that, he had to.

'Yes, even Vanessa,' he said slowly with grim self-mockery. 'Crazy, eh? But then something happened to show me what a real woman was like, to bring to the surface an ache that had been with me for eight long years. You were hostile, unfriendly and fiercely antagonistic, breathing fire and brimstone at every turn, and I knew that I still felt the same as I had at twenty-three. That you were the only woman I would ever love.'

'Logan——' she stretched out her hand for him to stop '—don't say these things; you don't really mean them even if you think you do now. I've seen you with Vanessa, I watched you dance with her tonight. She's everything——'

'—you're not,' he said softly, 'and I've thanked God for it. White satin opposed to black lace, pure feminine loveliness at the side of tawdry, cheap worldliness. It wasn't intentional but the dresses you both chose tonight were symbolic of everything I feel. I know you don't trust me, that you barely like me, but you're the one chance I have of making anything worthwhile of my life, Melly. I'm asking you to let me in. I know you want me physically and we could build on that——'

'Don't, Logan.' If he spoke one more word in that husky deep voice, looked at her for one more second, she would betray herself, fling herself into his arms and promise anything he wanted to hear. But how could she believe all he had said? She had seen Vanessa leave his room that night in England, watched the sensual blonde fling herself at him day after day. There would be other Vanessas even if what he was saying about his ex-wife was true, and could she trust him, really trust him, not to succumb to their female wiles? How did she know? How could she be sure? And he hadn't spoken of anything permanent. What if he grew tired of her once the initial novelty had worn off and the hunter had snared his prey? It would destroy her, in every way it would destroy her. Because if she went to him, opened up her heart and her body to this man, for her it would be a total, utter giving of self with no going back.

'I need you, Melly.' His voice was a low groan and the moment he touched her a wild, primitive desire sprang to life. And that, strangely, gave her the strength to remain outwardly cold and unresponsive in his arms. Because if she gave in to him now, followed the dictates of her heart, he would rip it out at the roots. And she couldn't think when he was near like this, he had said too much for her to absorb it all, she needed time. As his kiss became more intimate, plundering the inner haven of her mouth, it was sheer torture to remain still. She wanted to arch against him, feel the hardness of his body against hers, hear him groan her name in an agony of need. And then, just when she knew she was lost, she was free again.

'That's your answer?' he asked raggedly, his breathing harsh and uneven. 'This coldness? Well, is it?'

'Logan?' The familiar voice polluted the air like a flow of thick sour cream and as Logan swore once, viciously, she slipped past him to run across the small courtyard, past Vanessa who had just opened the door, and into the crowded nightclub with her heart thudding and her head pounding.

She stumbled along to the tiny ladies' cloakroom at the back of the nightclub, utterly unable to face the others at that moment. But that wasn't to be the end of it. Even as the door closed behind her it opened again to reveal Vanessa framed in the doorway, her mouth a thin white line of malignant rage and her eyes malevolent. 'It appears I interrupted a nice cosy little tête-à-tête out there?' she spat nastily as she closed the door and leant her back against it, effectively shutting the two of them in the small room. 'Well, don't think you'll have him for long, my dear sweet innocent little flower. You might seem to have all the winning cards right now but it won't last, I'll see to that. And if you take him you take Alexandra too, do you know that? He's ridiculously fond of the brat for some reason.'

'Dee's a beautiful little girl,' Melly said icily, in stark contrast to the other woman's vitriolic rage.

'Oh, come on, you don't have to pretend now when he can't hear you,' Vanessa hissed tightly. 'Kids are bad enough normally, ghastly little creatures with grubby noses and whining demands——'

'If you felt like that, why did you have one?' Melly asked grimly even as her legs were shaking at being on the receiving end of such sheer unadulterated hate.

'Because I wanted Logan,' Vanessa said immediately. 'I still do.'

'You're mad.' As Melly stared into the other woman's eyes she wondered, for a moment, if Vanessa really was quite literally unbalanced.

'Oh, no.' Vanessa straightened up from the door, smoothing the black lace slowly over perfect hips. 'Not mad. I just know what I want and make sure I get it, that's all. Now Giles can appreciate that. In fact he's very keen to be more than appreciative.' The cat eyes narrowed scornfully at the open disgust on Melly's white face. 'Oh, spare me the righteous disapproval, please, we're not all made of such noble material as you, darling, but then probably you don't have my opportunities either.' She smiled cruelly. 'But Giles will do for a time, until Logan tires of you, that is. And he will. When he can have any women he wants, why should he stay with you, after all?'

'Or you?' Melly asked shakily.

'Oh, but I don't expect him to be faithful, darling.' She spoke the word as though it was obscene. 'There's no reason why he can't have his fun like me, and now that Alexandra is older, when it looks as if things may be sorted out medically——'

'And what about the lost years?' Melly asked grimly, the trembling that the other woman had induced swept aside by sheer burning rage. 'Those important baby years when she needed a mother, when Logan had to be everything to her? How are you going to replace those?'

'I wouldn't even try,' Vanessa said disdainfully as her eyes narrowed still further. 'Logan is the only thing that matters to me.'

'But you don't love him.' Melly stared at her bitterly. 'If you did you would have stayed and tried to help him through the bad times, if not for your daughter then for him.'

'I want him.' Vanessa smoothed her hair before opening the door. 'He is the only man I've ever known where the wanting hasn't lessened, in fact I want him more now than I did when I first met him. Bow out gracefully now, darling, save yourself a lot of trouble.'

She let her eyes run scornfully over Melly's slender figure in the white satin. 'You just haven't got what it takes.'

Melly sat for long minutes in the cloakroom before joining the others and, when she did, the rest of the evening forever remained a blur in her mind, Logan's face, cold and uncomprisingly severe, the only thing that stood out from the hazy fog that had settled on her senses.

The next few days dragged by agonisingly slowly, made worse by Logan having disappeared on an unexpected trip to America, and on the day before they were due to leave Paris she was in her room packing when the telephone rang.

'Melly?' Paul's voice was instantly recognisable. 'How are you?' She shut her eyes briefly. Not now. Please, Paul, not one of your boring telephone conversations about your mother, your work and goodness knows what *now*. She had been unable to think about anything but Logan since the night at the nightclub, half expecting, half dreading that he would ring her from the States and then being disappointed when she heard nothing, flailing herself for her stupidity. Why should he ring?

'Fine, Paul, how are you?' she answered politely.

'I thought you were going to ring me at the beginning of the week?' he said with the slight whine in his voice that any divergence from a strict routine always produced.

'I've been busy.' She was too weary to offer any excuses, her voice flat. 'Besides which there was no news.'

'I thought we could go out for a meal when you get back,' he said after a moment's cool silence to let her know her attitude was not appreciated. 'I'll ring you, shall I?'

'I'm going to be busy when I get home, Paul.' She took a deep breath before continuing. If nothing else, the disaster with Logan had told her she could never willingly endure another tepid date with Paul. 'Let's just leave things for a few weeks.'

'Melly?' This time his voice was distinctly put out. 'What does that mean? It's that Steer fellow, isn't it? What's been happening with him?'

'Paul, this isn't going to get us anywhere,' she said firmly as her stomach lurched at the confrontation. 'I just don't want to make any arrangements, that's all. We're friends, aren't we? Can't I just——?'

'Friends?' Now his voice had a definite nasty note in its rather high pitch. 'It *is* that Steer fellow, isn't it? Have you slept with him, is that it?'

'I'm not going to discuss this with you any further,' she said tightly. 'We've had some nice times, Paul, but there was never anything beyond friendship between us and you know it. We had never discussed the future at all.'

'But I assumed...' His voice trailed to a halt. 'You fitted in so well with me; I thought——'

'But perhaps I don't want to fit in well with anyone,' Melly said sharply. 'And to be honest, I was quite aware that you saw me if and when it suited any arrangements with your mother.'

'But you didn't seem to mind,' he said indignantly. 'You never said.'

'Well, I am now.' She took a deep hard breath. 'I'd like us to continue to be friends, Paul, OK?'

'I'll talk to you when you get back,' he said frostily. 'Goodnight, Amelia.'

Ow! She grimaced to herself as she replaced the receiver. Amelia? But she had to let him know where he

stood. And Logan? She shut her eyes tightly as hot tears
seeped under the lids. What was she going to do?

As she walked down to breakfast the next morning her
eyes scanned the hotel dining-room quickly, but only
Giles and Alfred were seated at the table sipping coffee.
'Logan's not able to get back,' Giles said without pre-
amble as she reached them. 'He phoned from the States
last night. He's arranged a car to meet you at the airport
and take you to pick up the cat and then take you to
your flat. OK?'

'Thank you.' She smiled and sat down, wondering if
her face was as numb as her mind was. He'd had enough.
He'd said so. This was an easy way of bringing the matter
to a tidy conclusion. And she couldn't blame him, not
really. If she believed him, *if*, he had bared his heart
that night and she had all but trampled it in the dust.
But did she? And as she looked across at Giles chewing
stolidly on a piece of toast she knew the answer she had
been fighting for days. It took quite a man to take on
a handicapped baby by himself when his wife didn't want
to know, and even more to carry on with the commitment when he found out the child wasn't even his.
He was rich, very rich. He could have installed Dee in
a nice comfortable home somewhere to ease his conscience and provided a nice fat monthly cheque as salve
to any guilt feelings. But he hadn't. And why? Because
he had loved that tiny scrap of humanity battling with
any number of things that could have killed her. He had
loved her and he had fought for her because that was
the sort of man he was.

How could she have been so blind? She shut her eyes
tightly for a moment and then took a sip of scalding
coffee to force back the tears. She either accepted what

he had told her about Vanessa and everything else, or made up her mind he was a degenerate liar, and her heart had been trying to tell her head for days, weeks, what sort of man he was. She seen him in action in business, with Vanessa, and what she had *seen*, actually seen, had all been good. Why Vanessa had been in his room that night she didn't know, but when he had come to see her a few minutes later he had been fully dressed, not in a dressing-gown or as though he had retired for bed. So maybe... Maybe he hadn't been in there or maybe he had merely sent her away immediately she had arrived. She would never know now because she had lost the opportunity to ask him, along with the right to reach out to him. And suddenly that whole episode was pathetically unimportant.

The flight home was uneventful and the car was waiting as promised. As Logan's house came into view she hoped, desperately, that by some miracle his car would be there, that she would get a second chance. But only a strange daily answered the door, Marmalade in her arms and the cat box at her feet. Dee, and even the faithful Mrs Sturgess, were nowhere to be seen.

On the silent drive back to her flat Marmalade seemed to sense her despair as he nuzzled his big body into her lap, his huge green eyes staring into her face for a long moment before he rubbed his furry cheek against her soft skin.

'Oh, Marmalade, I've made such a mess of everything...' she whispered into the thick fur. She couldn't cry now, not in front of the dour uniformed driver who peered at her every few moments in the mirror from the front seat. But her heart was breaking. Could people survive agony like this and go on? she asked herself miserably as her flat came into view. Of course. It was life.

'No need for that, miss.' The driver had carried her bags into the flat as her arms were full with cat, refusing the generous tip with a little shake of his head. 'The governor has been more than generous, don't you worry.' And then he left, shutting the door behind him, and she was alone. Really alone.

# CHAPTER TEN

SHE was sitting curled up in front of the fire in her nightdress with Marmalade prowling restlessly about the flat in a way he never had before when the front doorbell rang piercingly. She glanced at her watch. Eleven o'clock! And no one knew she was home yet—she'd only been in England a few hours, after all.

She padded anxiously to the door and called softly, 'Yes, who is it?'

'It's me.' Her stomach took a nose-dive into her feet at the same time as her heart jumped into her mouth, and it took her a few seconds to get her body in order before she could move.

'Logan?' She was going to faint, she thought weakly, breathing quickly as she put a hand to her pounding heart.

'Of course.' There was that slightly irritated note in his voice now that worked better than any smelling salts. 'I can slip my passport under the door if that would make you feel better.'

'But you're in America,' she said faintly.

'Are you doing this on purpose?' There was definite steel encasing his voice now and she moved to open the door quickly, her eyes moving up to meet his as she saw him framed in the doorway, impossibly handsome, devastatingly delicious and *here*.

'Hello, Melly.' He smiled and her heart went into hyperdrive. 'We've got a problem.'

'A problem?' He was dressed casually in a black leather jacket and loose trousers that sat on the big body in a way guaranteed to cause heart failure. The only problem *she* had was how to stop herself leaping wholesale into his arms.

'A problem.' He gestured to the hall beyond. 'Can I come in?'

'Yes, yes, of course.' As she followed him into the small lounge she found she was trembling and prayed he hadn't noticed. She jerked the belt of her dressing-gown more tightly round her waist. Breathe deeply, Melly, she told herself as the butterflies in her stomach did a war dance. There's obviously a difficulty at work, that's all.

'What...? What's wrong?' she asked nervously. 'Is it Giles——?'

'Damn Giles.' The ice-blue eyes fastened on Marmalade, who had stopped the pacing and settled on Melly's chair in front of the fire where he lay purring ecstatically. 'I'm afraid you may have a paternity suit on your hands.'

'A...' Her voice trailed away as she tried to take in what he had just said. 'A paternity suit? I don't understand?'

'To put it quite plainly, Marmalade has abused my hospitality,' he said quietly, his face deadpan. 'It appears Tabitha is—how do you say?—with kittens.'

'No!' She stared at him before her gaze flashed to Marmalade who had stopped the purring and seemed to be listening intently. 'Logan, are you sure?'

'Quite sure.' He moved a step towards her until he was a breath away. 'And I was wondering, does a sin of that enormity wipe out my past transgression? You do admit it's serious?'

'I...' She stopped abruptly, unable to read his face.

'I've been in America, you see, with Dee. The operation was brought forward a couple of months as they felt she was ready. It was a complete success, she's going to be fine.' He swallowed hard. 'With appropriate therapy she'll be walking, running in months. It was the last hurdle, Melly.'

It took a minute for his words to sink in and then she did spring at him, her face alight. 'Logan, oh, Logan.' And he caught her, whisking her up into his arms and swinging her around and around as he held her so close she could hear the pounding of his heart.

'I have to get back. Mrs Sturgess is with her now. But——' he paused, his face torn with conflicting emotions of intense longing, pain and sheer exhaustion '—I wanted to tell you, I don't know why, and Marmalade's activities seemed the perfect excuse...'

'I know why you had to tell me.' She looked up into his dark face, still within the circle of his strong arms, and took a long hard breath. Truth time, and if she did get hurt, if he left her after a brief fling, well—at least she would never regret that she hadn't been brave enough to reach out for what she wanted when it really counted.

'You do?' The room seemed to be waiting as the air grew still and as he looked down at her, a faint hope in the beautiful blue eyes, she blessed Marmalade and his hormones.

'It's because I love her,' she said softly, 'and I love her father too.' She chose the word deliberately because, in everything that mattered, Logan was Dee's father.

'Melly?' He had frozen, his eyes desperate with desire. 'Don't say it if you don't mean it, you don't have to. I can be patient, I'll work at making you trust me——'

'I do.' And as she said it she knew it was true. It would be enough to be with him: the future would take care of itself. 'And I love——' But he had claimed her mouth, the blue eyes blazing with fire as his mouth opened over hers and he pulled her into his hard taut body with scant consideration for the delicacy of her bones. And the kiss was fiery, fierce, taking her into a world where the only reality was his hard masculine shape and strong arms, the touch of his lips and the sensations they produced. He had been holding back before, she realised that now, as his tongue demanded greater intimacy, flicking into the hidden contours of her mouth and producing a blissfully melting sensation in her limbs that was irresistible.

'I love you, my darling...' He raised his head to stare into the velvet brown of her eyes. 'I've always loved you, you have to believe that. When Vanessa said she was pregnant I went mad for a time, thinking of you, but I couldn't walk out on her. If I'd only known...' He groaned softly.

'But you wouldn't have Dee then,' she reminded him gently, her heart thudding.

'Will you marry me?' As he said the words, her heart stopped and then raced on at a furious pace. 'Will you, Melly?'

'Logan...' As she surfaced from the next kiss she managed a shaky laugh as she gazed up into his face. 'You've decided you can't bear my name a minute more?'

'Not a minute.' He pulled her into his body more securely and she shivered as she felt his arousal, hard and strong, against her softness. 'Mrs Amelia Steer will do very well though. And you will be married in white, with bridesmaids, the whole thing.'

'That's not necessary.' She gazed at him adoringly. 'I only want you.'

'You'll have that always, my love.' He kissed the tip of her nose and moved her gently from him as she pressed into his body, his voice suddenly dry. 'But unless you are prepared to shock Marmalade, I need some distance between us. I can only take so much, Melly, and right now I can't believe my luck. I came here in fear and trembling——'

'Not you.' She looked at him lovingly. 'I don't believe it.'

'It's true.' He wasn't smiling now. 'And another thing, and then we'll never mention it again. I meant what I said about Vanessa. I haven't slept with her since Dee was born. That night at my house, I didn't even know she had been to my room until you said. I was downstairs in my study working on some papers. When I questioned her about it after I left your room she admitted she'd been there and I asked her to leave. I told her how I felt about you and that I wasn't prepared for her to act that way. She left within minutes.'

'Logan...' She reached out her hand to touch his hard face. 'I'm sorry for not listening.'

'You are now.' He smiled slowly.

'I want you.' She moved back into his arms, her heart in her eyes.

'And I want you.' His voice roughened and he turned away, his profile taut and hard. 'But we are going to wait, Melly; we're doing it right. I want everything with you to be perfect because you are perfect. You always have been to me.'

Marmalade stretched lazily on the chair and then jumped down carefully, his big green eyes alight with satisfaction. It had taken some time but he had sorted out these strange human creatures most adeptly, all things considered.

He purred to himself as he strolled into the kitchen for his saucer of milk. He'd told Tabitha everything would be all right. This would be a good lesson for her for the future in leaving things to him. He lapped the thick creamy milk thoughtfully. After all, he was a family man now, had to set an example.

The purr deepened. Yes, he had handled the whole situation very well, if he did say so himself.

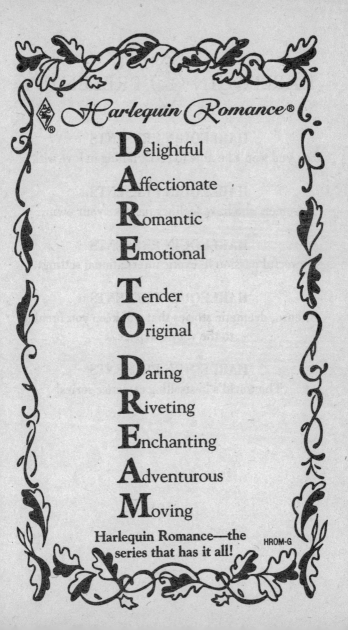

*Harlequin Romance*®

**D**elightful

**A**ffectionate

**R**omantic

**E**motional

**T**ender

**O**riginal

**D**aring

**R**iveting

**E**nchanting

**A**dventurous

**M**oving

Harlequin Romance—the
series that has it all!

HROM-G

# HARLEQUIN  PRESENTS®

**HARLEQUIN PRESENTS**
men you won't be able to resist falling in love with...

**HARLEQUIN PRESENTS**
women who have feelings just like your own...

**HARLEQUIN PRESENTS**
powerful passion in exotic international settings...

**HARLEQUIN PRESENTS**
intense, dramatic stories that will keep you turning
to the very last page...

**HARLEQUIN PRESENTS**
The world's bestselling romance series!

# ◈ *Harlequin*® ◈ *Historical*

If you're a serious fan of historical romance,
then you're in luck!

Harlequin Historicals brings you
stories by bestselling authors, rising new stars
and talented first-timers.

Ruth Langan & Theresa Michaels
Mary McBride & Cheryl St.John
Margaret Moore & Merline Lovelace
Julie Tetel & Nina Beaumont
Susan Amarillas & Ana Seymour
Deborah Simmons & Linda Castle
Cassandra Austin & Emily French
Miranda Jarrett & Suzanne Barclay
DeLoras Scott & Laurie Grant…

You'll never run out of favorites.

Harlequin Historicals…they're too good to miss!

HH-GEN

# LOOK FOR OUR FOUR FABULOUS MEN!

Each month some of today's bestselling authors bring four new fabulous men to Harlequin American Romance. Whether they're rebel ranchers, millionaire power brokers or sexy single dads, they're all gallant princes—and they're all ready to sweep you into lighthearted fantasies and contemporary fairy tales where anything is possible and where all your dreams come true!

You don't even have to make a wish...Harlequin American Romance will grant your every desire!

Look for Harlequin American Romance wherever Harlequin books are sold!

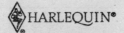 **HARLEQUIN®**

## *Not The Same Old Story!*

 **HARLEQUIN PRESENTS®**
Exciting, emotionally intense romance stories that take readers around the world.

*Harlequin Romance®*
Vibrant stories of captivating women and irresistible men experiencing the magic of falling in love!

**HARLEQUIN®**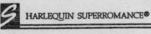
Bold and adventurous— Temptation is strong women, bad boys, great sex!

**HARLEQUIN SUPERROMANCE®**
Provocative, passionate, contemporary stories that celebrate life and love.

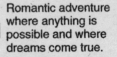 **HARLEQUIN AMERICAN ROMANCE®**
Romantic adventure where anything is possible and where dreams come true.

**HARLEQUIN® INTRIGUE®**
Heart-stopping, suspenseful adventures that combine the best of romance and mystery.

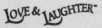 **LOVE & LAUGHTER™**
Entertaining and fun, humorous and romantic—stories that capture the lighter side of love.